To Come and Go Like Magic

KATIE PICKARD FAWCETT

Alfred A. Knopf
New York

THIS IS A BORZOI BOOK PUBLISHED BY ALFRED A. KNOPF

Visit us on the Web! www.randomhouse.com/kids

Educators and librarians, for a variety of teaching tools, visit us at
www.randomhouse.com/teachers

Library of Congress Cataloging-in-Publication Data
Fawcett, Katie Pickard.
To come and go like magic / Katie Pickard Fawcett. — 1st ed.
p.   cm.
Summary: In the 1970s, twelve-year-old Chili Sue Mahoney longs to escape her tiny Kentucky hometown and see the world, but she also learns to recognize beauty in the people and places around her.
ISBN 978-0-375-85846-8 (trade) — ISBN 978-0-375-95846-5 (lib. bdg.) —
ISBN 978-0-375-89538-8 (e-book)
[1. Country life—Kentucky—Fiction. 2. Family life—Kentucky—Fiction.
3. Kentucky—History—20th century—Fiction.] I. Title.
PZ7.F2697To 2010
[Fic]—dc22
2008052188

The text of this book is set in 13-point Perrywood MT.

Printed in the United States of America

February 2010

10 9 8 7 6 5 4 3 2 1

First Edition

For Michael and Dylan

And in loving memory of my parents,
Charles and Luverna Pickard

And the stars keep on moving—
no one can tie them to one place.

—Charles Wright, *Appalachia*

Leaving...

Momma's ironing on the sunporch when I break the news.

"Someday I'll leave this place," I say. The glider creaks when I give it a push.

"Where you going?" She looks at me with about as much concern as if I'd told her I was going to Brock's store for a Coke.

"Not sure," I say, putting my eyes on my painted

toenails. Aunt Rose spent the weekend with us and polished my nails Hot Geranium to match hers. I imagine these red toes walking down some wide tree-lined boulevard in a faraway city. The *where* is not important. I've never been anyplace but here. How can I have a *where*?

"People don't leave Mercy Hill," Momma says, laughing her *you don't know what you're talking about* laugh as she swipes the iron across Pop's white shirt, giving it a lick and a promise.

"Why not?"

She shakes her head. "Grass is not always greener on the other side of the fence," she says, sliding the hot iron carefully around each button.

"I don't care," I say. "I want to see what it looks like, see if it feels the same and smells the same someplace else." I'm thinking fresh smells, like perfume and new-car vinyl and strange food scents in a city full of fancy restaurants. Not like here. Not like Mercy Hill's coal smoke and sawdust and fields of cow manure fertilizing the corn. Momma's eyebrows arch the way they do when she's trying to fill in spaces with her black Maybelline pencil. "Grass is grass," she says. "One side of the fence is as green as the other."

Momma does not understand that the color of grass has nothing to do with it, that all the fences in the world separating here from there have nothing to do with it. Leaving is all that matters.

Outside these plastic porch windows the winter sun is white-hot and the bare maples and elms shudder in the slapping wind. Dried-up honeysuckle vines twist and dip along the fence top, barely hanging on to life. In the spring Pop will take off the scratched-up plastic windows and slip in screens, but today the backyard is a blur. It's like looking through water or into a dream world from some other place and time.

 Then and Now . . .

A year ago life was hunky-dory, as my aunt Rose says. A year ago we were the right size for this house. Momma; Pop; my brother, Jack; and me. Three bedrooms, two porches, and a dusty attic full of junk. A year ago my sister, Myra, was married to Jerry Wilson and lived in Jellico Springs. Uncle Lucius lived on Sycamore Street with his young redheaded wife, Gretchen. A floozie from way back is the way Pop describes her. With Uncle Lu going on seventy and her not even fifty, Momma says things were bound to happen the way they did.

The whole world can change in a year.

One morning Uncle Lucius woke up and found Gretchen gone. She'd run off with a traveling vacuum-cleaner salesman named Vernon Wright. Uncle Lu still laughs sometimes and says, I guess I was Mister Wrong. Then he goes out back under the sour-cherry tree and throws up.

Uncle Lu didn't want to sleep at his own house anymore, so Pop and Jack set up an old, wobbly bed frame in our attic, and Momma bought a cardboard chest of drawers at the Kmart in Jellico Springs and put yellow curtains on the tiny window. From that attic window, with Jack's binoculars, I used to watch redbirds sitting in the bare winter trees along the riverbank. Now the attic's off-limits. My uncle has to have his private space to moan and stomp and talk to himself, shaking my ceiling so much the overhead light fixture jiggles with last summer's dead bugs in it.

If the changes had stopped with Uncle Lucius, maybe it wouldn't have been so bad. But next came what Jack calls the *aftershock*. My sister, Myra, showed up at the front door with a suitcase, saying Jerry Wilson had run off, too, and she had a baby on the way. All this news, the good and the bad, spilled out in one long breath. Myra couldn't bear to sleep alone in *her* house either, so she moved in with me. Now she and her round belly with the baby-to-be take up most of the double bed, and every night I hang on to the edge, afraid to move. If I kick in my sleep and hurt the baby, it could end up loony or something.

Pop says everything will work out in its own time, but he spends *his* own time working at the hardware store away from it all. Three days a week Momma sells dresses at Donna's Dress Shop, and Jack practically lives at the ball fields—football, baseball, track. Any field will do. Meanwhile, I get to listen to Myra cry and my uncle curse the dogs. Our two dogs, Old Tate and Foxy Lady, live in a chain-link pen with identical white doghouses. Uncle Lu says those dogs are better off than he is.

English Becomes Geography . . .

I like school enough, but it's nothing special. I get mostly Bs and don't crack a book. Except to read stories, that is. My favorite spot in the whole school is the back row of stacks in the library. During morning study hall I sit on the floor in front of the radiator, smelling books and listening to the hot water sluice up through the pipes.

I like stories about people who are not real and places

that are hard to imagine. Anything can happen in a book. But Mrs. Sturdivant didn't let us read much literature last semester. She said we had to do grammar double time. "You butcher the English language down here," she said, emphasizing *down here* like it was a bad word, instead of just saying *Kentucky*. Mrs. Sturdivant's from Chicago, where people talk proper without doing grammar double time.

But now she's gone. She's having a baby, like Myra, except hers is coming in two weeks' time and she's still got a husband. We helped pack up her pictures and baby magazines and carried the boxes to her car because her doctor says she's not supposed to lift anything heavier than a loaf of bread.

We're all talking and laughing and Zeno Mayfield's trying to stand on his head in the back corner near the lockers when the substitute, an old gray-haired woman, walks in the door a full five minutes after the bell. Zeno calls her Granny. Right out loud, too. "Hello, Granny," he says, but she doesn't answer. He says she can't hear, but I see her smiling to herself.

Miss Matlock says she's going on seventy-one years old. She'll be seventy-two next year on the same day as the bicentennial, she says. The Fourth of July. And America will be two hundred. There'll be fireworks and picnics and parades everywhere.

Miss Matlock lives on Persimmon Tree Road five houses from us. I've seen her puttering in the garden, but she never talks to anybody. She's new to Mercy Hill, been here just a little over a year, even though Pop says she grew up in that same house back in the day. He doesn't say what day.

"I once taught seventh grade in Jellico Springs," she says. But that was in another lifetime, she tells us, a time when teachers were still allowed to hit you with wooden paddles one minute and pray with you the next.

"The Middle Ages," Zeno says.

Miss Matlock pauses in her introduction, gazes out the window.

After two years of teaching she went off to see the world, she says. The world is her favorite subject. She has never taught grammar, but she can teach anything in a pinch. And we all know the principal was in a big pinch trying to find a last-minute replacement for Mrs. Sturdivant, who had insisted that she was just getting fat until everybody could tell the difference. Fat does not collect in one spot the way a baby does.

Fifteen minutes in the classroom and Miss Matlock takes down our poster of HOW AND WHEN ADVERBS and pins a world map to the bulletin board. She points to the map with her ruler and covers up the printed names with her free hand. What's this green country? Which ocean is this? How many miles do you think it might be from here to here? Peck. Peck. Her ruler jumps across oceans and continents. We're all dummies.

"Who cares," Zeno Mayfield says from the back of the room. "What's it matter?"

"Hmmm . . ." Miss Matlock takes a pen from her bag, opens a little composition book with pink lilies on the cover, and looks over her glasses at Zeno. "Your name, sir?"

Sir? Everybody laughs.

Miss Matlock waits until Zeno spells his name.

"A most uncharacteristic name," she says. "It has potential."

Everybody laughs again and Zeno turns red and squints his eyes like he's looking into the sun.

Chile, the Country, Spelled Wrong . . .

I was named after the wife of a Civil War soldier, a Union man who almost died in my great-great-grandmother's bed. Why Grandma Sudie decided to take mercy on that poor shot-up man and the others who followed him is still a mystery. After all, my great-great-grandpa Buster was off fighting the very men she was trying to save.

The story goes that this soldier was out of his head for days, calling for a woman named Chileda, so that name got passed down and Momma picked it up and attached it to me. She says it's the only thing left from that time. The stone skeleton of Grandma Sudie's old house is still standing at the top of Mercy Hill, the mountain that gave this town its name, but the floorboards are rotted or missing, and in summer the milkweed grows four feet high where the old parlor used to be.

Pop didn't particularly like the name Chileda, so he nicknamed me Chili and that's who I am. Chili Sue Mahoney. Brown-haired, green-eyed, and skinny as a rail. Sometimes I wonder what it would be like to be somebody else, somebody blond and red-cheeked and cute as a button. Or black-haired and purple-eyed like Elizabeth Taylor used to be in those pictures Myra keeps in her *Scrapbook of Stars*. Or to just have a name like Elizabeth that takes its time rolling off your tongue.

But I'm Chili Pepper. Chili with Beans. Hormel. That's what Zeno Mayfield calls me and he smiles and shows his crooked teeth like an idiot. I prefer to be like Chile, the country, I say. Exotic and foreign and far, far away. I'm Chile, the country, spelled wrong.

The Penguin Bird on Blue Ice . . .
Three o'clock on a sunny February Thursday. The school-bus doors fold open and I get off, plop down my books on the front-porch swing, and turn back around and start walking. I don't want to go in that house and deal with Uncle Lu and Myra. Not today. So down Persimmon Tree Road I go, imagining what it would be like to keep walking until these brown winter hills disappear and every path and stream and gulley I know is gone. What would a place like that look like?

At Miss Matlock's old house a musty scent from the boxwood hedge swirls in the air like a strange perfume. Suddenly a straw hat bobs above the bushes. Something sharp and shiny, a pair of clippers, reaches over the top of the hedge and snips the air. It's too cold to be wearing straw hats and clipping bushes.

"Who's there?" A screechy voice slips through the boxwood.

I stop like a soldier at attention. Zeno says old Miss

Matlock's crazy. Last spring she threatened his cousin Clydie—said she'd cut him up in little pieces and throw him in the Cumberland River if he didn't quit riding his bicycle through her purple phlox plants. She opens the gate now and steps in front of me with her hands on her hips like a judge, but she's my same height, eye to eye.

"Who are you?" she asks.

"Chileda Sue Mahoney," I say. "I'm in your third-period class."

She flips up the dark plastic shades attached to her eyeglasses. "Oh yes, yes, yes," she says. "Mahoney. Bick Mahoney's girl?"

I nod.

"Come inside my gate, Miss Chili." She motions with her tiny bird's-foot of a hand, all skinny and wrinkled and purple-veined. But her sharp blue eyes are steady and glassy clear. She says: "Have you ever been around the world?"

"I've been to Jellico Springs," I say proudly, even though Myra's old town off the interstate is nothing special, just a bump in the road.

She laughs and takes off her straw hat, freeing that bushel of wild gray hair. "Come on in," she says, "we'll take a trip."

A trip through an old house? I think it but don't say it.

It smells like a library. Tall bookcases line the parlor walls and every table and chair is stacked with yellowed newspapers and magazines, leaving hardly enough room to sit or stand. With every step we take, the wood floors creak like bones breaking.

Momma would not tolerate this mess for one minute. She'd nail down those loose boards and burn the old papers and make everything spick-and-span clean. But Miss Matlock seems to fit in with the clutter, and I'm drawn like a magnet to its mystery.

She drags a rickety ladder from a closet and asks me to climb up and take down a thick red and black book from the top shelf.

I'm on the fourth rung, feeling the ladder start to wobble.

"¡Hola! ¡Hola, muchacha!"

I turn quickly and have to grab on to the bookcase to keep from falling. A large green parrot is sitting on the back of the sofa. His head is turned to one side and he's looking up at me. Miss Matlock clicks her tongue and the bird swoops across the room and perches on her shoulder.

"This is my Ivan," she says. "Ivan the Terrible."

"What did he say?"

" 'Hello,' " she says. "He was greeting you in Spanish."

"Spanish?"

"Ivan's from the jungles of Ecuador," she says. "He's bilingual."

"Bi . . . ?"

"He speaks two languages." She laughs. "Well, let's say he speaks a few words in two languages."

After clearing a spot for the red and black book on the coffee table, Miss Matlock and the parrot go off to make tea.

I hear her singing in the kitchen and the tinkling together of silverware and dishes. A few minutes later she's back, carrying a flowered teapot with steam escaping in smoky threads and a tray of sugar cookies dripping with white icing.

"This is Miss Chili," she says to the bird on her shoulder. "Chili, Chili, Chili."

The bird cocks his head and opens his beak slightly but doesn't say a word.

Miss Matlock sits and creases back a page in the big book.

"Now we begin," she whispers, as if she's about to read a sacred story or reveal some ancient secret.

But it's only a book full of pictures. Black kids with big round bellies are as naked as jaybirds. Momma would never approve of me gawking at pictures of naked people, especially these boys with enormous bellies.

"They're hungry," Miss Matlock explains, her lips quivering at the edges.

How can anybody that fat be hungry?

She turns the page. "Perhaps we should look at something more pleasant."

We explore the wide streets of Paris, France, and green islands with palm trees in the Pacific Ocean and penguin birds in Antarctica. Something about those bird eyes gets to me. They're hard and piercing, like a dagger to the heart. I know if I stay in these hills, I'll never see a real penguin bird standing on blue ice with a milky sky behind him.

"I gotta go," I say. When I jump from the couch and head for the door, I hear Miss Matlock's old feet shuffle behind me.

"Where you going?" she calls after me. "Come back sometime. We've got lots of places still to see."

On the porch I stop and turn around to thank her for the tea and she's standing with the screen door wide open. In that drab gray dress and white apron she doesn't look at all like a teacher. She looks more like a propped-up paper doll, a maid or a grandma posing in a fancy dollhouse doorway, waiting for the paper-doll family to come home.

I walk awhile, skip awhile, past telephone poles with their lines humming in the silence, sending voices from here to there. At the lane to our house I start running as fast as I can, feeling lighter with every breath. Light as the powder on a moth's wing. Light enough to float away.

Sand Without Stones . . .

Miss Matlock brings a Ball jar of sand to school so we can see and feel the African desert. She says the tiniest of these particles floats across the ocean from Africa and lands on our doorsteps.

Willie Bright raises his hand and says this looks like plain old riverbank sand. "It's got little rocks in it," Willie says. He sits with his arms crossed and eyes glued to the teacher. His shoes have holes and his pants are too short and his curly yellow hair looks like it's never seen a comb.

Willie Bright is a welfare. He lives with his momma and little brother and sister and a crinkly old grandma on a hill across the meadow from our house. His daddy ran away when his little brother was born. I guess if you're that poor, one more kid won't turn the grass any greener.

At bedtime the desert is still on my mind. I dream of a camel walking down Persimmon Tree Road with a man in a blue robe perched like a king between the two humps. When they get to our porch, the man asks for a drink, so I run to the kitchen and bring back a pitcher of ice water. After he takes a long swig, he points to the place where the river and the mountains are supposed to be, but there's nothing but a long stretch of sand with the road running through it.

"Do you know what's out there?" he asks, blinking at the sun.

"Sand," I answer. "Sand without stones."

The camel rider laughs like some wild animal, and his black eyes dance across my skin in a peculiar way that makes me feel uneasy. He bends down till he's almost at my face and I can feel his hot breath blowing in my eyes.

"All the dreams in the world are waiting there," he says, "but you must watch out for the wind. It can take your breath away."

I see only sand and sky and so much light it hurts my eyes. I want to ask more about the desert, but I'm in one of those dreams now where you work your mouth but the words won't come out.

"Come with me," the man says, his blue robe blowing in the breeze.

In real life I'd never go near a strange man, but a dream is a dream.

When the camel starts to turn away, I grab on to the flying tail of the man's robe and we head down a road that stretches through the desert like a thread in a sandbox.

Suddenly, the second we're about to cross over a high dune where I won't be able to see Mercy Hill anymore, I wake up. Catching my breath. Trembling.

 Willie Bright...

Willie Bright says he never believed in Santa Claus, not even when he was in kindergarten. Not for one minute.

"Who d'you think brought all those presents?" I ask. I'd wondered about flying reindeer and all that stuff, too, but Momma explained that Santa Claus was the good spirit of Christmas and if I didn't believe in the good spirit, I might not get anything, so that kept me on track for years.

Willie Bright laughs and says he didn't get presents. Not even one.

I tell him it's hard to imagine an empty floor under the Christmas tree.

"Ha," Willie laughs. "Not for me. We've never had a tree."

We're at the school-bus stop and it's so cold I have to keep my hands in my pockets.

"I forgot my gloves," I say, changing the subject away from Santa Claus.

Willie tells me he doesn't have any gloves to forget. So I look for still another subject. We're the only ones at the bus stop. The other kids have all been taken to school because it's too cold to stand outside.

"Pop would've taken me to school," I say, "but he had to go to work early because Mr. Simms is out of town." When Mr. Simms is away during the cold weather, the school bus is always late. It's like the driver plans it that way.

Willie has to stand in the cold and the rain and the snow every day. They don't own a car because his mother can't drive. She takes fits. When a spell comes over her, she falls down right where she is and doesn't even know she's alive.

I look up now and see Willie grinning at me as if I've made a joke about Pop driving me to school.

"If my momma ever got behind the wheel of a car, she'd probably kill herself or somebody else," he says. "Tell *that* to your Santy." His face is pinched up and his nose is red and when he laughs, he shakes all over. Mostly it's because he's cold.

 ad Habits . . .

"Don't hang around with welfares," Pop says. "You'll learn bad habits."

"What habits?"

"Habits," he says. "I don't know."

"You don't know?"

Pop takes a deep breath and lets it out in a puff. "You'll learn to expect something for nothing," he says. "You'll want to depend on other people in order to eat."

"Like Uncle Lucius and Myra?"

"No, no, no!" he shouts. "Not like Lucius and your sister. They're different."

"How?"

"Go get ready for school," he says. "I'm trying to read my paper."

Pop's at the table with the *Courier-Journal* opened on his left and the *Knoxville News Sentinel* on the right. He likes to see who's saying what about important people.

When it's time to vote, Pop knows both sides and he always votes the man, not the party, he says. But no Democrats. No women. Pop has limits.

I'm at the doorway when I decide to turn around and ask him a difficult question.

"What if I was to run for president some day? Would you vote for me?"

He looks up and laughs. "You?" he says. "You got a C in math the last six weeks."

"So?"

"So . . . you couldn't be president of anything. Not in a hundred years."

I don't like math. I hate numbers. Numbers are not like words. Words have something to say; they go places, do things. Miss Matlock says words can change the world. You won't see any numbers do that.

Collections . . .

We've been best friends since kindergarten. Ginny Murphy, Priscilla Martin, and me. We ride bikes, babysit, and do jump-rope team together. The "three Ms" is what our teachers call us. Pop says "three peas in a pod."

Ginny collects teen magazines and Priscilla collects ribbons for her hair.

"What do you collect, Chili?" Priscilla looks at me with her pale gray eyes.

It's stone quiet. Just the bells in the church tower ringing noon. Ding. Ding. Ding. Twelve times. I wait.

"Words," I say.

"Words?" Ginny looks at me like I'm joking.

I collect words. They don't have to be long or hard to spell, but they do have to be words we don't use around here. *Concoction.* That's the latest word in my red notebook. I think about mixing stuff in a big tub—herbs and spices and oils and colored water. A concoction. When I use a word that we don't say around here, Ginny gives me *that* look. I make her tired, she says. I make her want to . . . she can't think of a word. Sigh, I say. I make you want to sigh. Ginny rolls her eyes, looks at the clouds.

I collect words, but they don't do anything . . . yet. It's like if Momma put up tomatoes and stuck the jars in the cellar and we never got around to eating them for a long, long time.

The Corner Store...

Brock's store is on the corner where Persimmon Tree Road ends and Main Street begins, and they sell anything you want. Bread and milk and candy and meat. Mrs. Brock makes baloney sandwiches at lunchtime for the state highway men who pave the road in the summer and scrape snow in the winter. Even when they're working somewhere else, the men come to Brock's to get lunch because it's cheap. Not like a restaurant. They pay for the baloney and bread and Mrs. Brock makes the sandwiches for free. "No tips," she says. "We don't take tips." She says this in a half whisper when Mr. Brock is standing nearby.

One day a city man traveling to Louisville stopped and bought a sandwich and left a dollar tip and Mr. Brock followed him all the way out to his car and propped the door open till the man took his money back. "No tips," Mr. Brock said.

In the back room of Brock's store the men play dominoes every day. Ralph Becker, Benny Moss, Will Epperson, and sometimes Little Clyde Cummings. Little Clyde is six feet tall, but he's Little Clyde because his pop is Big Clyde, even though Big Clyde is short and fat. The men laugh and slap their legs and ask Mrs. Brock to bring this or that, Juicy Fruit gum or chewing tobacco or a baloney sandwich, and she runs here and there at top speed like one of those little cars you push until the wheels are spinning so fast it can go all the way across the room without stopping.

After jump-rope practice we stop at Brock's and buy Bazooka gum and a Hershey bar to split three ways for Ginny, Priscilla, and me. In the back room the men holler for cold Dr Peppers, and Mrs. Brock rushes with our change and gives us back four quarters instead of four nickels and slams the cash-register drawer before we can say anything. Ginny says we could buy another Hershey bar and get four extra sections each. Or we could leave Mrs. Brock a tip. Priscilla puts the quarters on the counter beside the meat slicer where only Mrs. Brock is likely to see them, and we run as fast as we can out the door and down Persimmon Tree Road.

irds and Boys...

Twice a week, Monday and Thursday, I go to Miss Matlock's house after school and we travel to places in her books—the mountains of Mexico, the Nile River, the sandy beaches of Indonesia. I tell Myra and Uncle Lucius I'm going to the library. If they knew I was at the old woman's house, they'd tell Pop and he'd say I couldn't go back. Even though she's my teacher, some people think Miss Matlock's crazy and others just don't like her. It has something to do with her running away when she was young.

Ginny and Priscilla agree with the grown-ups. Ginny says that anybody who hates a place enough to run away automatically becomes an outsider. So I don't dare tell them about going to Miss Matlock's house or about my own thoughts of leaving Mercy Hill.

So what if people roll their eyes and shake their

heads at Miss Matlock? I don't think she cares one bit. She has other stuff to care about, like her books of the world and her pictures and stories of the places she's seen. And she cares about keeping her bushes trimmed properly and talking to Ivan the Terrible.

Ivan says *Chili, Chili, Chili*—always three times when I come in the door and again when I get up to leave. Miss Matlock says it only took a week to teach him my name. He's a smart bird and not terrible at all.

"Perhaps I'll bring Ivan to class one day," Miss Matlock says. "If I can trust Mr. Mayfield to not annoy him."

"Zeno annoys everybody," I say. "He lives to annoy people."

Miss Matlock smiles. "We must find a way to make this boy a bit more palatable," she says.

"What's that mean?"

She presses her finger to her lips and studies on this for a while. "More appetizing," she says. "Like adding chocolate icing to a plain cake."

Palatable goes in my red notebook, but I sure wouldn't put Zeno Mayfield in the same category as chocolate icing.

$\mathcal{M}$iss Hart, Queen of Homeroom ... "Do NOT smudge your paper," she says, tapping my fingers with the ruler. "The machine cannot read the test if you're messy."

Miss Hart, queen of homeroom. That's what Zeno calls her. She's in charge of spring testing in the cafeteria for grades six, seven, and eight. We're all bunched together under the fluorescent lights, half of them blinking and trying to go out, so it's hard to concentrate.

"People in other places make really good scores," she says. "We cannot let them beat us."

The page is a dance of words. *Treacherous. Prudery. Gesticulate.* If I could write them in my red notebook, I could collect a million from this test alone. We don't talk like this, so how can they expect us to answer the questions? How can we beat the people in other places?

At the next table Ginny winds a strand of blond hair tightly around her finger like this might stir up some brain cells. Priscilla slips off her shoes under the table and taps her bare feet on the tile floor. Everybody's moving, stretching legs, scratching arms, twisting from side to side. Everyone except Willie Bright, and he's bent over with his face down close to the test booklet, like he's having a hard time seeing the words.

Ginny and Priscilla were upset earlier because they got put at a table with Willie and two sixth-grade welfares. It will make them look like dummies, Ginny said. There ought to be rules. But Miss Hart didn't make the rules. She says these are simply tests to show our strengths and weaknesses (whether we're regular or talented or dumb is what she really means and everybody knows it) before we sign up for next year's classes. Still, in the end, you can choose any classes you want; the scores don't matter. I take a deep breath and keep working.

Don't turn the page until the buzzer sounds. Read fast, answer *a, b, c,* or *d.* Two may be right, but only one is the best. Zeno Mayfield says 75 percent of the answers are *c,* so if you always answer *c,* you get 75 percent right, which is like getting a C on your report card. Pop does not like Cs.

Math and science in the morning; history and reading in the afternoon. I like the reading best, but I'm tired by the time we get to it. My eraser's gone, too, beaten down to the last bit during math. When I try to erase, the metal rim of the vanished eraser leaves a dirty smudge outside the box.

"Don't go outside the box!" Miss Hart marches up and down the aisles, looking over shoulders, stockings swishing against her legs.

I try to keep my mind on a long passage from some book called *Pride and Prejudice*. It's about a little village in England and there are five girls, sisters, all tangled up in some kind of love story. The questions are hard. *What is the hypothetical situation set up by the author?* If I only knew what *hypothetical* meant . . . *What is the author's belief as indicated . . . ?* I guess and go on.

Ten minutes before last bell we're finally printing our names on the back sheet, filling in personal information—grade, birth date, school—and I put the post-office-box number on the wrong line and have to erase, making a streak across the whole address section. Miss Hart stops and taps my desk with her ruler.

"The eraser's gone," I say.

She grabs my pencil and breaks off the eraser end. *Snap!* Throws both pieces in the trash, takes my test, and strolls up the long aisle like she owns the school. All that work and no post-office-box number. My test will probably get lost and I'll have to wait another year for a chance to beat all those people who make really good scores. I feel the others turn in their chairs and wait to see if I'll cry, but I clamp my teeth together, top to bottom, so not even a thread could slide through.

It's a long time before the bell rings.

R oscoe . . .

"Your uncle Roscoe died," Momma says. She sits at the foot of my bed and wrings her hands till they're red. She's told Myra and Jack, and now she says she's here to prepare me.

"For what?" I ask. I didn't really know Pop's brother.

She says they're bringing Roscoe to our house for three days.

"How can Uncle Roscoe come to our house if he's dead?"

Momma explains that this is how it's done. The dead lie in the living room and all their friends and even some of their guilt-ridden enemies come to view them.

"Why's he coming *here*?" I ask Momma. "Why don't they keep Roscoe in West Virginia where he lived?"

"This is his home," Momma says.

"*Our* house?" I ask. Uncle Roscoe's never lived in our house, and I can only recall him visiting us twice.

"Mercy Hill," Momma says. "This is his true home."

"What's a true home?" I ask. How can a true home be one you never even visit? I sit up in bed and twiddle the fringe on the blanket. I've heard stories that Uncle Roscoe's wife, Big Nan, is bossy. She spanks the kids, Little Nan and Humphrey, with a yardstick every time they do the least thing wrong and refuses to even accept Lenny as a family member. He's Roscoe's oldest kid, by some other woman. Big Nan runs a tight ship, Pop's always said. Now she's casting Roscoe overboard, sending him home in a box.

"A true home is where you started out," Momma explains. "That never changes."

I look around at my blue curtains and peacock bedspread and dark wood floor. I look out the window where the bare sycamore branches shiver in the morning breeze. Momma's shivering, too, and I reach over and pat her on the shoulder.

"I'll help clean the house," I offer.

"Yes," Momma says. "We'll make it pretty for Roscoe's homecoming."

When Momma's gone, I picture myself in a far-off country living amongst strangers. I'm from Mercy Hill, Kentucky, I'll say, knowing that no matter where I go, that will never change.

 R_{oxy March...}

The undertaker backs his long black car up to the front porch and brings in Uncle Roscoe with baskets of white roses and yellow gladiolas and tiny pink carnations. Momma places vases on the coffee table and the mantel and the television set. Blooms are everywhere, blossoms and green leafy ferns smelling up the house.

People will be coming and going day and night, so I have to wear a good dress and my patent-leather shoes. It's like church around the clock.

I see a fancy-dressed woman walk through the door looking like she's lost.

"Uncle Roscoe's in the living room," I say.

"He's not *really* here," she says, shaking her head. She's wearing a green suit with sharp-toed, high-heeled shoes to match, like the women on television. I picture myself in a suit like that, walking into a fancy office building with windows all around. But I wouldn't have that purse she's carrying. It looks like animal hide. Some poor alligator or crocodile or a bunch of lizards had to die so she'd have a place to put her lipstick.

"He's right over there," I say, pointing to the casket sitting in front of the window. It's brown and shiny with silver handles and a satin lining. From where Uncle Roscoe is perched, he could see the sun rise above the maple trees if he were alive.

"That's nothing but a cold body," the woman says, dabbing at her eyes with a Kleenex. She tells me Roscoe's gone, he's flown away, like a pretty bird that sits on a telephone wire and sings for a while and then takes off.

"What's your name?" I ask, wanting to know more about any woman who could imagine my pale-faced, plump uncle Roscoe as a pretty bird.

"Roxy," the woman says. "Roxy March."

"I've heard that name," I say. She's the one Roscoe loved before he went off to the war. But then he came back and took up with a foreign dancer—Lenny's mom—who died and left him to marry Big Nan and ruin his life. That's how the story goes.

A bunch of women from church descend on Roxy March, fussing over her green suit and shoes and animal purse. They say Roxy is better off without Uncle Roscoe. . . . He would have kept her in the hills. . . . Now she's a legal secretary in Cincinnati and that's almost like being a lawyer, even better than being a lawyer in Mercy Hill.

"Look at her!" A blond woman's head bobs up and down above the others. "Would you just look at her!"

They've come to view Uncle Roscoe but can't keep their eyes off Roxy March.

71 Beech Street . . .

Strangers sleep in my bed. Old men curl up with their hats over their faces, women stretch out in their stockings and pretty dresses, and little snotty-nosed kids snuggle under my covers.

"I wouldn't dream of sending anybody to a hotel," Momma says. She gives my room to Big Nan and Little Nan, and Jack's to Humphrey and Lenny when they get to the house.

"Let's go to my house," Myra offers, even though she's not been back to that house since Jerry Wilson disappeared.

All the way down the interstate highway my sister taps on the steering wheel like it's a drum. Finally, we whirl round and round beneath the overpass and pull up in front of 71 Beech Street. We sit in the car and look at the front-porch chairs turned over on their sides and the storm door standing open. The house looks creepy or sad. I can't tell which.

Myra makes me a bed on the couch in her living room, but I can't sleep. I hear her sniffling in the bedroom and don't know if she's crying about Uncle Roscoe or Jerry Wilson or about being back in this lonely little house again. Maybe she's just tired of carrying the baby-to-be around all day and night.

Lenny...

You can turn away stray cats and strangers, but you can't turn away family. After the funeral Big Nan took an extra suitcase from the trunk of her car and plopped it on the driveway. She had Little Nan and Humphrey to raise, she said, and didn't have the time nor the energy for a teenaged boy who belonged to some other woman. Lenny's mom, Uncle Roscoe's first wife, died the day he was born.

So Lenny moved in with my brother, Jack.

It'll never work. Jack plays baseball and football and his friends are rough and vulgar. Basically, he's everything Lenny can never hope to be.

Still, Lenny starts out trying to act tough. "I killed

one momma and drove the other one crazy," he says. But his mouth twitches at the corners and it looks like any minute his legs might collapse.

"Lenny's mother was a dancer from New York City," Momma tells me. "She talked with a strange accent, but she was as pretty as a picture."

"Roxy March is pretty, too," I say, remembering the woman with the green reptile bag who came to see Uncle Roscoe.

"Well . . . yes," Momma says. "Roscoe was certainly handsome in his day. He could have any girl he wanted."

"Did he *really* want Big Nan?"

Momma laughs. She says Roscoe had the bad luck to fly around all the pretty roses in the garden and then land on a cow pie.

Church, Chimps, and Eyes . . .

"Get up!" Pop yells from the bottom of the stairs. "Time to go to church."

He stomps up the stairs and sticks his head inside my doorway. "Are you ready?"

"What's it look like?" I say, throwing off the covers. Pop's always asking questions when he already knows the answers.

"Don't sass," he says. Beside me Myra groans and covers her head. She'll be excused again from going to church.

We sit together stretched out in the pew. Lenny, Jack, Momma, and me. Pop's up front singing in the choir. He throws back his head and I can hear his voice above the others in the refrain of "In the Sweet By and By."

We shall meet on that beautiful shore.

I hope Pop's not thinking about meeting up with Uncle Roscoe anytime soon. Our house already seeps with sadness. Uncle Lu lost Gretchen and Myra lost her no-good husband, Jerry Wilson, and Pop lost Roscoe. But Momma says Lenny's lost more than anybody. He lost his parents and his home and his half brother and sister. But I say there is one good thing: Lenny lost Big Nan, too.

The preacher paces behind the pulpit with the Bible in his hand, his white shirt wet with sweat and sticking to his back. He stops and wags a finger at Frances Perkins sitting at the organ.

"We did not spring from chimpanzees!" he shouts.

Miss Perkins teaches science at Mercy Hill High School and this drives the reverend crazy. Twice he's tried to get the city council to burn those new textbooks with pictures of ape-looking men, but they're afraid the government will take back its education money. Without that money Mercy Hill couldn't even buy toilet paper for the school bathrooms. That's what Pop says.

Lenny shakes his head and bends across Momma's lap to say something to me. "Darwin again," he whispers.

When Lenny was unpacking his suitcases, he showed me drawings of hairy cavemen in a book about Charles Darwin. They do look like apes, but so far I've been agreeing with the preacher. I've never seen a real person who looks like a monkey and I've seen some ugly people in these hills.

Suddenly the preacher shouts a string of strange words, leaps into the air, and comes back down on the edge of the stepping-up place. He tumbles out of the pulpit and onto the organ.

"Lord have mercy!" Miss Perkins screams and the whole choir stands up at once like they've been told to rise.

The preacher's face is red and pinched up in pain. He jerks like he's been stung by a hornet and keeps calling out to the congregation in a language that nobody understands. Momma says he's talking in tongues.

"Hallelujah, he's alive!" Little Clyde Cummings shouts from the back of the church. "Call the ambulance!"

Frances Perkins shuts off the organ and sits weeping loud enough for everybody to hear. Finally, some men come and carry the preacher away on a stretcher with the sirens blaring.

It's quiet in the car on the way home and I'm thinking about last summer when the traveling carnival came through town and Pop gave me money to buy a bag of peanuts for the monkeys. They'd crack the shells and slip off the hulls before popping those nuts into their mouths. I remember their round, beady eyes full of water.

"The preacher shouldn't get so upset about monkeys," I say.

Momma shrugs. She's sitting in the front seat with her back to me. "Those apes do look a little like people, don't they?" she says.

I look over at Lenny, but he doesn't say a word about Darwin and the ape-men.

"Maybe it's their eyes," I say. "It's the way they stare at you."

 ncle Lucius and the Kites ...

The March wind is fierce. Every morning Uncle Lucius goes to the meadow with a cart full of kites and sets them flying until the sky is filled with color. Diamond shapes, boxes, some with long tails and others that swirl round and round like whirligigs. All day long Uncle Lu sits in his fold-up chair hidden amongst the grasses between the mountains and the river. He sits with his kites in the air against the blue sky, working the strings, as if this were a real job. When the sun sets, he brings them down again and loads them onto his two-wheeled cart and heads back to the house, his hair a ball of cotton torn apart in the March wind.

At breakfast I ask Uncle Lu what he's doing in the meadow when the kites are flying all by themselves.

"Thinking," he says.

"I wish I could stay home all day and fly kites," I say.

I grab my backpack and head for the school bus, imagining all those colors blowing across the sky and all that time to do nothing but think. Somehow I've got

to drag myself through math and history before English/
geography, which is the only class I've ever had that goes
by too fast.

All day the rain starts and stops, pours and drizzles, the
sky gray and cold-looking like a slate dump. No kite flying today. At last bell we all get soaked running from the
classroom building to the school bus, but the bus driver
won't turn on the heat. He's wearing a green jacket with
a hood, says we need to remember to bring our own
jackets, and makes it sound like the rain's our fault.

Halfway home the sun comes out and melts the gray
clouds with its heat. In patches high above the holes in
the clouds, the sky is blue like the ocean must be.

At the supper table Pop unfolds the newspaper and
hands Lucius a section, trying to get him interested in
what's going on in the real world, but Uncle Lu stares
out the window and sips his coffee. He doesn't even care
about what's going on in this room.

After a while he gets up, walks into the front hallway,
and pulls something from his coat pocket. A long cylinder
wrapped in blue tissue with a red ribbon. He smiles and
hands it to me, even though it's not my birthday or anything.

I peel off the paper and find a cardboard kaleidoscope
with colored gemstones inside a tiny peephole.

"It's great, Uncle Lu. Where'd you get it?"

"From a hippie," he says.

"A hippie?"

"Down at Brock's store. He was walking the Appalachian Trail end to end, and he got off in Virginia just so he could see Kentucky."

"Really?" Pop looks up from his paper.

"That man had hair clear down to here," Lucius says, swiping his hand midway across his back.

"He just gave this to you?" I ask. The kaleidoscope looks brand-new.

Uncle Lu shakes his head. "I bought it," he says.

Pop puts down his fork and looks hard at my uncle. "How much did you pay for it, Lucius?"

Uncle Lu shrugs. "Gave him what I had in my pocket."

Momma groans at the other end of the table. I know Uncle Lu went into town this morning to cash his Social Security check. That money was supposed to last all month. "Surely . . ." She looks at Pop and sucks in her breath.

I feel like a worm crawling around in the dirt.

"You don't have *any* money left?" Pop asks.

I look from Momma to Pop. "It's not my—"

"Shush," says Pop, wagging his finger at me.

"I've got plenty money in my wallet," says Uncle Lucius. He takes it out and spreads bills on the table. "I gave that hippie my pocket change."

Pop looks relieved, and Momma reaches over and

pats Uncle Lu on the arm. Veins are popped up on his bony hands like little blue rivers. I look over at him and smile, and Uncle Lu smiles back.

When supper's over, I take the kaleidoscope to the window and aim it at the sky where the sunset's brightest. The plastic colors fall into perfect shapes, one after the other, like glass flowers, gumdrops, tiny kites.

On Being Different . . .

"I'm gonna be working in the garden when planting time starts," says Willie Bright.

"You are?"

"Yep. It'll be a lot of responsibility. I probably won't have much free time."

We're waiting at the bus stop and I see the school bus in the distance creeping along like an old yellow turtle. I don't recall the Brights ever having a garden and I've known Willie for as long as I can remember. My family's been here since my great-great-grandparents Buster and Sudie built the house on Mercy Hill. Willie claims his family's been here even longer, but I don't think he can prove it.

He's poor and I'm not. He knows it and I know it, but mostly we've not talked about it. Lately, though, he's been saying stuff, reminding me that we're not alike. Sometimes I think he likes being different, but not especially being poor. Maybe he'd like to be different in some other way. Still, I'll bet he doesn't know the first thing about planting a garden.

"Where do you get corn plants?" I ask.

"You shell the dried corn," he says. "You drop the kernels in furrows."

"What about beans? Do you pick beans once or more than once in a season?"

"More than once," he says. "Bean plants bear all summer."

Lucky guesses. "How do you plant potatoes?"

"With the eyes up." Willie grins and looks down at his feet.

"It's hard work," I say. I tell him how the sun gets blistery hot in the garden and the chiggers bite and dirt clogs up under your fingernails. I do this *every* summer.

He looks at me and shrugs. "I'll do okay," he says. His eyes are ablaze in the sun.

"Maybe," I say.

When the school bus stops, Willie Bright steps back and lets me get on first.

 he Wisdom of Spring...

Rain and freeze and thaw. Icy winds and warm winds, dry winds and winds full of rain. Every day is different; every day is the same. The grass is green, fluttering in the wind, and wild purple violets bloom around the stumps and rocks.

We're out walking and talking, Aunt Rose and me, searching for wildflowers.

It's the time of year when people living in the hollows come to town and stretch their legs in the sun. They're heathens, Pop says. Those little kids are growing up in places that even God forgot.

Every year VISTA workers tote them out of the hills and into town. Volunteers in Service to America is what they're called, rich northerners thinking they can save the poor. Pop says the mountain people run loose and spit on the sidewalks and claim they're here to get what the government owes them.

The third Wednesday of every month the commodity

truck comes to town handing out free food—big jars of peanut butter and blocks of yellow cheese and boxes of powdered milk with no-brand, plain brown wrappers, but the ones who get commodities don't like the no-brand food. They sell everything for money to buy Camel cigarettes and Cokes.

Sometimes Aunt Rose buys commodities from Mountain Bessie, an old woman who collects from the others and sells stuff from the back of her pickup truck just outside the Piggly Wiggly parking lot. Rose puts the cheese through the sausage grinder with pickles and red pimientos and makes enough pimiento spread for a month's worth of sandwiches.

After the commodity truck's gone, the mountain people stand on the courthouse square smoking cigarettes and drinking Cokes and pretending the third Wednesday is like any other day and they are like any other people. But it's not any other day and they're not like any other people.

We're not either, Pop says. We're sure not like those newscasters on the six o'clock programs. Whether we like it or not, we're more like the mountain people.

While we walk, Aunt Rose has been stooping down to pick periwinkle flowers. She hands me a purple blossom.

"See that star?" she says, pointing to the center of the tiny bloom.

I bend over for a better look. The purple star, out-
lined in white, is as perfect as if it had been drawn with
a ruler. Aunt Rose says you can't really know a thing until you've looked at it up close for a good, long time.

Secrets, Songs, and Bad Dreams...

I'm putting on my coat to go to school when Myra waddles down the stairs on the verge of tears with her pink
robe dragging on the floor behind her. She had a dream
about Jerry Wilson, she says. He was in a car wreck on
some curvy mountain road and was all alone and waiting
to be rescued. She wants Momma to stay home from
work today, she says, rubbing her belly. She can't be alone.

I'm already late and need lunch money, but Momma
ignores me and tries to get Myra settled down.

I look out the window and see the school bus stop at
the corner to pick up Willie Bright and then head down
Persimmon Tree Road without me.

"I've missed the bus," I say to Momma. "There it goes."

She looks at me like I'm from another planet.

Myra plops down on the couch and almost pushes

Lenny's cassette player onto the floor, but I run over and grab it while it's still rocking back and forth.

Last night Lenny set the cassette player on the couch arm so he could listen to his music and dance in front of the living-room mirror. He tapes songs off his transistor radio late at night when our stations close down and clear the airwaves. Then you can hear stations from far away—Chicago, Baltimore, Fort Wayne. But mostly they fade in and out and carry static. Lenny likes some show called *The Top 25*, every night at nine. Rock music. Ear-piercing music, Pop calls it. Some nights he sends Lenny out to the sunporch so nobody else has to listen to it.

Lenny tapes songs that our stations don't play—"Free Bird" and "American Pie" and "Riders on the Storm." He goes around the house singing: *I fought the law and the law won.* Uncle Lu wags his finger. You'd best steer clear of the law, he says. Lucius doesn't like "Gypsies, Tramps & Thieves" for the same reason. Not the kind of people to associate with, he says to Lenny, like these songs are about real people.

Lenny can dance better than most girls, but Pop says it's prissy. He makes him chop wood or clip the holly bushes or do some other ornery task when he catches him dancing. But nothing stops Lenny. It's in his blood, he says, because his momma was a dancer.

When Pop turns his head, Lenny dances with the ax or spins on his toes like one of those Spanish dancers, with the clippers snapping above his head. *Castanets,* he says, and I collect that word for my red notebook.

Now I walk in and out of the room listening to Momma and Myra.

"He was *doing it* with everybody in town," Myra whispers, like this is a big secret. You can see the disgust curl across her splotchy face. Everybody knows Jerry Wilson ran around with other women, but nobody ever said anything about it to Myra. That's just the way it is here. People like to talk about the crimes, but nobody wants to tell the victims. If you tell, you're the one they end up hating. That's what Aunt Rose says. She's seen it happen a million times.

"What's *doing it* mean?" I ask. I like to put them on the spot.

Momma looks at me like she could bite a nail in two. "Go upstairs to your room until I tell you to come down," she says.

"Yes, ma'am." I stomp up the stairs but stop at the top to listen. Pop will have a talk with the Wilsons, Momma says to Myra. Jerry Wilson's going to pay for this baby. That's the bottom line.

A long silence.

I hear water running in the kitchen. Momma will

make a pot of coffee and pour it down Myra. Coffee always makes the women feel better, but it makes that baby-to-be kick like crazy. Poor little thing. Smaller than a teacup and being drowned in coffee. The doctor tells Myra to drink milk, but she won't listen. Every night she lines up baby outfits on the bed, like crayons in a box, in every color except blue and pink. Will it be a boy or a girl? She stands and stares.

After a few minutes of thick, hot silence Momma comes to the foot of the stairs and looks up at me through the railing.

"Come on down and I'll run you to school," she says.

Sex Education . . .

Ginny sits on the thickest branch of the cherry tree. Priscilla's up one more branch, dangling her legs in Ginny's face, and I'm stretched out at a fork in the highest spot before the limbs get too weak to hold a person.

"She was half-naked when she ran into the woods," Ginny whispers.

"Who?" I ask. "Who was half-naked?"

Ginny frowns like I'm a dummy. "I said they didn't recognize her, Chili. It was too dark."

Priscilla repeats Ginny's story about some teenagers parked at night down by the river and the sheriff walking up and popping a flashlight in the window. The girl jumped out and ran into the woods, Priscilla says. They're both laughing, so I laugh, too.

"Chili doesn't know what we're talking about," Ginny says to Priscilla, and they look at each other like they're in some special club for two.

"I do, too," I say.

"You don't even know what *doing it* means," Ginny says, swinging down from the tree.

"I do, too," I call after her.

Priscilla gives me a pitiful look. "It's just sex," she whispers. "We're going to get sex-ed classes next year if the school board says it's okay."

I think about the *True Confessions* magazines I've seen in Aunt Rose's closet. Sometimes when she's busy cooking or hanging clothes on the line, I slip in and read the dog-eared pages. You can learn a lot of stuff from the dog-eared pages, maybe even more than from a sex-education class.

Priscilla and I take our time climbing down. Ginny's out of earshot, running ahead of us to Brock's store to buy blue raspberry Popsicles.

"Zeno Mayfield asked me to marry him," Priscilla says.

"What?"

"To pretend," she says. "He wanted to pretend we were married."

"Why would you do that?" I ask.

Priscilla says Zeno wanted to put his hand up her skirt.

"Yuck!" I imagine his dark, rough hands sliding up Priscilla's pale legs.

"Of course, I didn't let him."

"What did you say to him?" I'm curious to know how to handle such a situation.

Priscilla laughs. "I told him he could *pretend* he was doing it."

April Fool ...

I hate oral reports. I hate all those eyes watching me sweat and stutter and cough. I've memorized more about Harriet Beecher Stowe than anybody in the world needs to know, because Miss Matlock says that's the best way to get over the butterflies.

Before I get through the introduction, Zeno Mayfield

starts making faces at me. I can tell when Miss Matlock is looking down to write her remarks because Zeno's face switches from angel to pure demon. The others want to giggle, but they're afraid to. I look over all their heads to the back of the room, where Willie Bright sits in the last row with his hands folded on his desk, listening. I pretend I'm talking to Willie, telling him all about Harriet Beecher Stowe as if she's somebody I'd like for him to meet.

I dish out the facts and the theories. When Abe Lincoln met this woman, he said, "So you're the little lady who started this great war."

The girls look up as if called to attention, boys jiggle in their seats, Zeno frowns. I tell about *Uncle Tom's Cabin* and how Mrs. Stowe wrote about geography and travel, too. I can't see Miss Matlock behind me, but I imagine her looking pleased.

"I never heard of that woman," Zeno says without even raising his hand.

"Quiet," says Miss Matlock. "Wait until Miss Mahoney's speech is finished."

Speech? The boys laugh and make jokes until the teacher has to get up and walk the room.

My mind leaps over Willie Bright's head and through the gray lockers, across the mountains and rivers, all the way to the Civil War and back. Maybe my words take Willie there, too. He smiles at me the minute I'm done.

When the bell rings, Zeno Mayfield rushes up the
aisle and hands me a note. It says:

You are the prettiest and smartest girl in the
whole school.
Turn this over.

I look on the back:

APRIL FOOL!!!

Spring Floods and Rats of All Kinds . . .
Momma sets rat traps and puts out poison. The spring
floods bring rats that eat their way into the cellar and the
corncrib and the smokehouse.

For three days floodwater backs up and fills the
meadow, and when it goes down, it leaves the riverbank
a slippery mess. Crawdad castles collapse and the crea-
tures get trapped in the mud. Every day they dig their
way out with mud caked to their shelly bodies and leave
trails in the wet earth as they make their **way to the**

water. Along the bank where the ground is especially steep and slimy, it's easy to lose your footing and slide into the dirty river.

Myra says that must have been what happened to Jerry Wilson. He must have slipped and fell.

Two days ago Will Epperson and Little Clyde Cummings were fishing for catfish and found Jerry Wilson's car in a thicket at the top of the riverbank. It was stuck in the undergrowth and the kudzu vine was already halfway up the doors. He'd left a note on the front seat saying that he couldn't stand to live in this world any longer. It didn't say whether he just meant Mercy Hill or if he was talking about the whole planet. Myra won't admit it, but it doesn't sound like he slipped.

Pop shakes his head when we get the news, says this world has too many responsibilities for a man like Jerry Wilson, who didn't want any. He doesn't believe the sheriff's report that says Myra's no-good husband walked into the river and drowned and the floods came and washed away his footprints.

Momma and Myra cry and wring their hands and walk the floor, but Pop does not let go of one tear. He says he'll believe the sheriff when he sees the body.

Every day the Mercy Hill Fire Department drags the river, searching for a body that's been missing for ages, but they don't retrieve anything, not even a sock that belonged to Jerry Wilson. Pop says it's because the rat's not there. He'd bet his eyeteeth on it.

After jump-rope team practice, I go down to the river with Ginny and Priscilla to wait for the men to come back from their third search. Third time's a charm, Aunt Rose says. This may be the day they find the body. The floodwater has receded and the river's running calm and clear. New buds are popping open on the bushes and the birds are singing high up in the trees like nothing has happened. No matter what bad thing comes along, the world keeps on doing what it always does.

Overhead two airplanes make white streaks across the sky, one laid over the other like a big X, both flying south to Atlanta or Pensacola or maybe New Orleans, leaving their contrails across Kentucky. That's what Lenny calls airplane smoke. *Contrails.*

In the marsh behind us little sulfur butterflies float up from the weeds like a swarm of bees and beat their yellow wings against the sky. We watch and wait.

It's dusk when the men come back empty-handed.

"That body could be anywhere," Will Epperson says. "It could have been swept all the way to the ocean by now."

"Or to Denver or Sausalito," Pop says.

"Huh?" The men look at Pop like he's crazy.

Eating Poke Salad...

We're at the kitchen table eating poke salad greens that
Aunt Rose picked this morning and cooked all day until
the house now stinks to high heaven. Poke salad is poi-
sonous if it's not cooked right or long enough, but Aunt
Rose is an expert. She watched my grandma cook the
wild greens and learned how much grease to put in and
how high to keep the fire going to kill the poison.

"Not much poke in the woods anymore," Rose says.
"Barely enough for a good mess."

"Wonder what's happening to it?" Momma twirls the
greens around on her fork and takes a slippery bite.

"All this tromping up and down the hollows," Rose
says. "Going in, going out. Driving vehicles off the road
and into the weeds."

"The VISTAs," I say. "Must be the VISTAs." Everything bad that happens, happens because of the VISTA
workers. The old mule paths and coal roads are now full
of jeep cars driven by foreigners, mostly northerners

who don't know one thing about hill people. That's what Pop says.

"That bunch is just down here to get their faces on the television set," Rose says.

"Aren't they supposed to be helping the poor people?" I ask.

"Sometimes," says Pop. "But sometimes they make matters worse."

"Worse?" I'm wondering how the poor in these hills could get any worse off.

"A man can take everything you've got," says Pop. "But you've got to hold on to your pride." These city people are taking away all the pride, he says, making hill folks feel sorry for themselves and thinking they don't have a thing to offer this world.

"Do they?" Jack asks.

"Everybody has something to offer," says Rose.

"A few people do need the help," Pop says. "But this aid money's making the others as lazy as bess bugs."

"What's a bess bug?"

"Chileda, you ask too many questions," Pop says.

Momma picks up the mashed potatoes and passes the bowl.

"I saw Yellow Creek on the news last week," she says. "And what they showed was about as far from the truth as you can get."

"They pick out the worst shacks in the county," Pop says, "and they find some poor ignorant man or woman and ask them a bunch of stupid questions."

"The whole world will think we all live that way," Momma says.

"Who cares what they think?" says Lenny.

"It's a plain insult," Pop says. "Would they pick some slum in New York City and put it on television and say, 'THIS is New York'?"

"Maybe not," I say.

"Well," says Aunt Rose, "I wouldn't take one penny of free money. Not one red cent."

"A few people do need it," Pop says again. "You have to remember that."

"Who?" says Rose. "Who needs it?"

"That Bright family," says Pop. "They'd starve without it."

Rose shakes her fork at Pop. "If old man Matlock had paid Helena's pap like he should have back in the day, the Brights wouldn't want for nothing now."

"Who was old man Matlock?" I ask. And I'm thinking: Who is Helena and does this have anything to do with Miss Matlock or is it another Matlock?

"Change the subject," says Pop. "It's time to change the subject."

"But I didn't get my question . . ."

Pop looks over at me. "Have you memorized your Bible books?" he asks.

"Almost."

"See how many you can name now." He looks hard at me and I know my question will not be answered. Not now. Probably not ever.

"Genesis, Exodus, Leviticus, Numbers, Deuteronomy, Joshua, Ruth, First Samuel . . ."

"You forgot Judges."

"Judges?"

"Judges comes between Joshua and Ruth," Pop says. "Order's important."

"Miss Perkins says order doesn't matter that much."

"What kind of teaching is that?" Aunt Rose shakes her head. "That's just not right."

Timing . . .

I stand on the Brights' porch with a Tupperware full of yesterday's leftover poke salad. The old grandmother opens the screen door and peers up at me for what seems like a million years.

"It's just that Mahoney girl!" she calls back over her shoulder, and waves me inside.

I follow her through the living room and down the hallway to the kitchen, her walking cane tapping sharply on the bare floor. The house smells of mildew and burning wood. In winter the floors are cold, Willie says, and ice forms on the window panes so you can't see out in the mornings.

The two little kids are sitting at the kitchen table eating chocolate fudge from a pan that looks like it's just come off the stove.

"Don't eat it all!" The old woman cracks her cane against a table leg, causing the little girl to jump and drop her spoon. "They won't even let that candy get hard," she barks.

Willie's momma is ironing clothes by the stove, and she looks up at me and smiles. Behind her the wall is covered with glossy magazine pictures and advertisements stuck up with straight pins like the ones Aunt Rose uses for sewing—colored pictures of *Family Circle* cakes and pies and *Good Housekeeping* gardens. "Where's Willie?" I ask, handing the greens to the old woman.

"Got his nose in a book," she says, pointing to the window.

I look out and see Willie sitting under a maple tree in the backyard. He doesn't look up and I'm glad. Every time we have leftover food that's too good to throw away or feed to the dogs, Momma has me bring it to the Brights.

Mrs. Bright and the old grandma always say they're glad to get it, but I wonder how Willie feels. I wonder how I would feel if Willie brought food to our house?

The air is full of questions. I think about the story Pop wouldn't let Aunt Rose tell at the table, about someone named Helena and some old man Matlock not paying somebody and that having something to do with the Brights being poor. Maybe Pop didn't let Aunt Rose finish because it was just gossip. After all, there are lots of poor people in Mercy Hill. And there are lots of people like us who have a car and a television that works and money in the bank for an emergency. As long as it's just one emergency, Pop says, and not a big one. We're lucky, Momma always says, but Pop says luck is something you make.

"Go on out and say hello to Willie," Mrs. Bright says. She lifts up the iron and lets the steam hiss from it.

"That's okay," I say. "Momma said I had to come straight back for supper."

I'd just as soon Willie didn't know I was here. Maybe he doesn't even like poke salad greens.

In a snap I'm out the front door and on my way, taking my questions about the Matlocks and the Brights back home with me. Maybe I'll ask Aunt Rose sometime when nobody's around and enough time has passed that she can't remember Pop not wanting her to tell the story. Timing is important. Timing is everything.

 urry Who Sings . . .

Surry Nan Honeycutt sings in the shower. Zeno Mayfield walks around all day repeating this like it's a rhyme to remember. Miss Matlock says: "Is that your mantra, Mr. Mayfield?"

Everybody laughs. I write *mantra* in my red notebook, which I keep under my desk when I'm at school.

Brown-eyed, forlorn-looking Surry moved here from Tennessee. Her family is big, four sisters and three brothers, and they all sing. Surry plays the dulcimer, plucking strings that whine like her voice, sounding as lonely as Old Tate crying at the moon.

Surry does not even have a shower. They live in a shack near the new projects. The new projects have indoor bathrooms and shiny kitchens and backyard patios, but you have to stay on a list a long time to get a place there. The Honeycutt house has four rooms, a tiny kitchen, and a muddy backyard with a toilet down a path through the trees. It's full of spiders.

Black widows, Surry said. They can kill you with one bite.

She was just trying to scare us—the welcoming committee: Ginny, Priscilla, and me. The counselor sent us with a bagful of school supplies, a tin of homemade peanut-butter fudge, and a sugar-cured ham.

The minute we walked in the door, Surry's pop grabbed the ham out of Ginny's arms so hard the plastic packing ring caught on her friendship bracelet and snapped it off. He said Surry could talk to us for five minutes only, so we went to the front porch, where you can sit and look at the new projects across the street, twenty-five houses all alike with grassy lawns.

"It's like looking at pretty clothes in a store window," Surry said. She was rocking back and forth on the concrete porch floor like she was sitting in a rocking chair.

Five minutes on the dot her pop banged on the screen door and said we had to leave. But Ginny had to use the bathroom, so Surry took us to that little outhouse in the backyard and we took turns. She waited and fidgeted like she had ants crawling all over her. Bit her nails and hummed. Wouldn't look us in the eyes.

When it was my turn, I saw the spiders working on webs in the corners beneath the roof. They didn't look dangerous. They were just little brown spiders like the ones we have at home.

"Nope. They're black widows," Surry said. "They'll kill you in one bite."

Her eyebrows came together hard and her eyes finally found ours, but it wasn't really a scared look she gave us. Not of the spiders, anyway. Not of us, the welcoming committee. There wasn't one bit of real terror in those eyes until her pop yelled out the back window and said it was the last time he was going to tell her to come in the house.

We started for the road with our heads down, heard the screen door slam, and walked faster.

"DON'T COME BACK HERE!" It sounded like he was talking on a loudspeaker.

Two little boys running with a black dog through the projects stopped and turned around, thinking all that hollering was meant for them.

The Honeycutts sing on Mercy Hill's radio station every Sunday morning at nine o'clock. Surry plays the dulcimer and sings "Will the Circle Be Unbroken?" She writes the words to the song on the cover of her notebook from the welcoming committee bag:

There's a better home awaiting in the sky,
Lord, in the sky . . .

 histling in Africa ...

Whistling girls and cackling hens always come to some bad end. That's what Aunt Rose says.

The sun has already crossed the equator, so Pop said it was time to plant. Jack and Lenny hoed furrows in straight rows for the scraggly tomato plants Pop brought home from the hardware store. He gets a discount for the plants other people don't want. He says if you put your sweat into them, they'll be just as good as the top-notch plants, so that's what we're doing. Planting and sweating.

I start whistling. At first Aunt Rose thinks it's Jack and doesn't say a word. Anything Jack does is all right in Rose's eyes.

I keep following her down the tomato row, but when she turns around at the end, she catches me with my lips puckered.

"Just work," she says, "and don't whistle."

I look down at my dirty fingernails and envy Myra,

who doesn't have to help because she's looking after that baby, despite the fact that it's not even here yet.

The sun's going down fast and we've still got a bucket of plants to set. Rose talks too much and slows us down. She places each plant in the furrow and I come along behind her covering up the roots. Momma and the boys are doing the same thing in the next row and now they're way ahead of us. I start to lose my patience and that makes me want to whistle, but I bite my tongue and hold it in.

Finally, Momma and Rose head back to the house and leave us to water the new plants. In the open field with Rose gone I can whistle all I want to, but no good tunes come to mind.

"I wish I was at a Red Sox game," Jack says.

We play this game called "I wish" when we've been stuck with an ornery task and have to get it done fast. It's like birthday wishing without the cake and candles and it has to be something that we can't imagine ever doing for real.

"I wish I was dancing on Broadway," says Lenny.

We're supposed to keep the game going fast. I think hard, but no wishes come to mind.

Both boys stop watering and look back at me at the same time. If I don't say something fast, I'll be out.

"I wish I was whistling in Africa," I say.

Lenny laughs out loud, but Jack just shakes his head.

At the end of the row Jack picks me up and carries me piggyback all the way to the front porch, where Aunt Rose is sitting in the swing drinking iced tea.

"Chili wants to go to Africa," Jack says. "What do you think about that, Aunt Rose?"

I kick him in the side with my heel, but he can't even feel it.

"Hmph," Rose says, shaking her head full of beauty-parlor curls. "Why would anybody want to go off to some dangerous place like that?"

Lenny slips up behind us.

"To whistle," he whispers.

This time Jack laughs, too, and Aunt Rose looks at us like we've lost our minds.

Faces in the Clouds...

"What's the secret to happiness?" Miss Matlock looks over the room, snaps her fingers. "Don't hesitate," she says. "Say the first thing that comes to mind."

"Having fun," says Priscilla.

"Lizards and four-leaf clovers," says Zeno Mayfield.

"Hoofbeats," says Surry who sings.

Hoofbeats?

"I've always wanted a horse," she says, her face turning bright red. "One that can run faster than the wind."

Everybody laughs. "No horse can run that fast."

"What about you, Chili?" Snap. Snap.

"Distant lands," I say.

Ginny and Priscilla turn and look at me and frown. They are fully content right here in Mercy Hill, the center of the universe.

We each make a list of happy sights and sounds and smells. The redbuds and dogwood blooming pink and white on the mountains, blackberry cobbler, church bells. Wild grapevines to swing on. Jasmine flowers. Bobwhites singing in the trees. Faces in the clouds.

My list is different from the others, full of sights I've never seen, foods I've never smelled, sounds I've never heard. Happy sights and sounds and smells from pictures and stories of places faraway.

"Those probably aren't real," Ginny whispers, leaning across the aisle to see my paper. "Your list is not even real."

Outside the window there's a rabbit in the clouds, a rabbit with one enormous blue eye where the sky's coming through and a crooked smile that keeps getting bigger and bigger. Like it's laughing at us.

Opening Shots . . .

Lenny stands in the living room beneath the ceiling light, a white globe the size of a grapefruit hanging from a brass chain with a blue glass shade covering it like a hood. Flower designs cut into the blue glass let the bright light sparkle through. This fixture is one of Pop's favorites, bought at an antique fair on the Cumberland Gap. It's our spotlight.

We pull down the shades. Everyone's gone to Jack's baseball game except Lenny and me. I sit on the couch with the cassette player balanced on the arm next to the wall, singing along: *Chick-a-boom Chick-a-boom don't ya jes' love it . . .*

"Watch the clock!" Lenny shouts. When he dances, he forgets that time exists. Inside the glass doors of the big clock on the mantel a brass pendulum swings back and forth, ticking off the minutes above the Mars bars. Pop hides candy in the clock so he can have a snack when he stretches out in front of the television late at night.

Almost eight o'clock. I still need to write my essay on Marco Polo.

"Let's start over," Lenny says, stopping to take a breath. "How about the Who?"

He digs through the stack of cassettes and hands me a new one. After turning off the light, he waits for me to slip it into place and then run to the switch and turn it back on at just the right time. This is what Lenny calls an "opening shot." You have to get the timing right.

I slide in the cassette, snap the door closed, and get ready to push the play button.

"Wait, wait!" Lenny yells, and he takes off up the stairs.

I hear the door to the attic open and close. What on earth is he doing?

Before I can hardly breathe, he's back with Uncle Lucius's walking cane, the one Uncle Lu takes to the mountains to poke in the underbrush and run off snakes when he's searching for ginseng.

"What are you doing with that?"

"You'll see," he says.

Lenny points the cane and tells me he's ready. So I push in the play button and hurry to the light switch.

Perfect opening shot! Lenny holds the cane in place and dances around it.

The Who sings: *I can see for miles and miles and miles . . .*

Faster and faster. Round and round. He gives the cane a kick. Slides it under his arm. Whips it out and . . .

I can't stop it, can't get a word out. Lenny twirls the cane like a majorette's baton and hits the blue glass light shade, splintering it into a million pieces. They fall onto the wood floor in a circle around his feet, and for a moment it looks like Lenny's on a real stage surrounded by a thousand twinkling lights.

"We need a broom," I say, and I head toward the kitchen. Neither of us says a word while we're cleaning up. Lenny gets the vacuum cleaner to suck up the fine pieces and I start upstairs to write my essay on Marco Polo.

"My mother danced on a real stage with a real spotlight and music played by a live band," he says.

"I know." I turn and leave him staring up at that bare globe like he can wish it back together.

"Don't tell your pop," he says when I'm halfway up the stairs. "Maybe he won't notice."

"Maybe," I say.

I do my homework as quick as a snap and jump into bed, thinking Pop will discover the broken light shade the minute he walks in the door. But maybe not. I cross my fingers under the covers. Maybe he won't find out until Lenny's left home. Maybe I'll be gone by then, too, and he won't even remember what the light looked like when it had a shade.

The May Day Royalty Contest . . .
Every day at lunchtime the jars go up on a table outside
the principal's office. Alma Jo, the school secretary, sits at
a folding chair behind the table and watches the jars,
counts the money. Rolled-up dollar bills, silver, lots of
pennies. Each jar has a label with a photo and name of
the girl running in the May Day contest. The queen will
come from the high school, the princess from sixth
through eighth, and the miniature queen from elemen-
tary. Kindergarten and first grade have their own candidates for the Tiny Miss crown.

This contest has nothing to do with beauty or personal-
ity or good grades. It has everything to do with money. The
one with the most wins. So if you have money left over
from lunch, you can put it in the jars. Or you can bring a
donation from home or help wash cars at the Piggly Wiggly on Saturdays or buy big packages of jawbreakers and
Hershey's kisses at Dinky's Discount and sell the little
packages in the lunchroom for a lot more than they cost.

Priscilla and Ginny are both running for princess, along with five of the popular girls. They all sit together in the cafeteria at lunchtime. Since kindergarten we've had lunch together every day, but now I sit alone. Their table, the first one inside the door, is just for princess candidates. This is not a real rule, just Melody Reece's rule. I'll be glad when May Day is over.

I bring my lunch and enough money to buy milk. That's it. Every day Ginny and Priscilla ask if I've put money in their jars. I'm saving, I say. Maybe tomorrow. But it's a waste of money to "vote," which is what they call contributing money, for anyone except Melody Reece. Her daddy is the manager of the Piggly Wiggly store and he's put jars at every register with a picture of Melody wearing a crown that looks an awful lot like the May Day princess crown. Brock's store put up jars for Priscilla and Ginny, but the Piggly Wiggly gets a lot more customers, especially ones who actually buy stuff. Most of the people at Brock's are there to play dominoes. Anyway, they're old men who don't have money to waste.

I see Zeno stuffing his lunch money in Melody's jar every day, thinking he's going to be the next prince. The girls get to choose their escorts and every single one of them is crazy about Zeno, even though he's the most annoying human being alive.

Myra was the May Day queen when she was in high school. She wore a long white gown and rode on the back of a red convertible in the May Day parade. Momma has her picture sitting on the mantel above the fireplace.

I tell this to Willie Bright at the bus stop and he says: "If you were running, I'd put all my money in your jar."

"You don't have any money," I say.

"If I did have money and if you were running . . ."

"That's a lot of *ifs*," I say. "Besides, I'm not the princess type."

oments . . .

I'm helping Momma clean Uncle Lu's room while he's out fishing. It's a mess. Dirty clothes piled up in one corner waiting to be toted downstairs to the washing machine, opened pouches of Prince Albert tobacco lying around half-full, shoe boxes full of dried, muddy roots. Uncle Lu searches the mountains for all kinds of wild roots and seeds and flowers to make herbal remedies.

"Don't ever eat or drink any of Lu's mixes," Momma says.

"I'm not stupid."

"Chileda, I didn't say that. I simply—"

"I know, Momma."

She scoots the shoe boxes under the bed.

"I don't see how he sleeps with the heat up here," she says. "Why don't you go downstairs and bring up a fan."

I grab an armful of Uncle Lu's dirty clothes, head down to the kitchen, and drop the shirts and pants and holey socks on the floor in front of the washer. We don't have a dryer, so Momma has to hang everything on the clothesline out back. It's not too bad in the summer, but in the wintertime the clothes freeze and take forever to dry. Sometimes, when a whole week is wet and cold, we have clothes hanging inside all over the house. If Myra and Uncle Lu stay until next winter, we won't have enough room to move around on laundry day.

I bring up the fan and Momma makes a place for it on Uncle Lu's dresser. It feels cool as long as you follow the blowing air from side to side.

"How big was Grandma Sudie's house?" I ask. My great-great-grandmother died a long time before I was born and there's nothing much left of the family house on Mercy Hill.

"I thought it was a castle back then," Momma says. She's stripped Uncle Lu's bed and is putting on a fresh white fitted sheet. I get on the opposite side and stretch the ends around the mattress corners.

"It must have been huge!" I try to picture the old house from the tales she's told of kids running through the rooms and up and down the staircase. She made it sound like a party every day.

Momma laughs. "Not really," she says. "It just seemed that way because I was so small. Everything looks big to a little kid."

"Was it as big as the Matlock house?" I grab my side of the flat sheet and tuck it under the mattress without looking up, act like this question came right off the top of my head from nowhere.

"Oh no," Momma says. "The Matlocks were rich people."

"How did they get rich in Mercy Hill?"

"Coal," she says. "That's the only way anybody's ever gotten rich here." She slaps Uncle Lu's pillow and fluffs it up just so.

"Mr. Matlock was a miner?"

Momma laughs again, but it sounds like a put-on laugh this time. "I doubt that man ever went down in a mine," she says.

"Then how—"

"We're about done here," she says. "I need to get supper started."

"But why can't we talk about—"

Momma shakes her head. "Chileda, sometimes it's best to let sleeping dogs lie."

"What does that mean?"

"Leave the old stories alone. Let them be done with."

"But—"

"Besides," Momma says. "I was a little girl back then, so I wasn't bothered by all that coal business."

She takes up the dust mop and runs it hard across the floor. I wish I hadn't gotten her mind off Grandma Sudie's house. I like to hear her talk about living there, about all her brothers and sisters and cats and dogs, about being poor and rich at the same time.

"What did you like best about Grandma Sudie's house?" I ask now. "*Your* home."

She picks up the rest of Uncle Lu's clothes and stands looking out the attic window with the view all the way to the river. "Maybe the way the light fell through the kitchen window," she says. "I liked to stand in that patch of light in the early morning and just dream."

I start to ask about her dreams, but somehow this doesn't feel like the right time.

"Your grandma always said that you had to take hold of the moments that don't last long," she says. "That patch of light never stayed but a few minutes."

Momma stands now in the late light falling through

the attic window and I try to imagine her as a young girl standing in the bright morning sunlight of Grandma's kitchen. She starts to smile but doesn't look my way. She's smiling to herself. If I had a camera, I'd take her picture.

May Day Parade...

Melody Reece won the May Day princess contest. She jumped up and down when Principal Goodman announced it, hugging all the popular girls and acting like she was surprised to death. The rest of us sat there and watched. Ginny and Priscilla joined all the hugging even though they lost to Melody. They'd do anything under the sun to be in that group of girls. She deserved it, they said. I wanted to ask why but didn't. If you have money jars sitting all over town, it's hard to lose.

Then disaster struck at the May Day Eve queen's-court dinner. Priscilla walked in wearing the same pink dress as Melody Reece, and Melody's momma almost had to be carried out on a stretcher. These are my momma's exact words. Her garden club sponsored the dinner, so she had a front-row view of the whole thing. Everybody thought

Mrs. Reece had a right to be upset. After all, she was the first May Day queen back in 1955. Her lilac-colored dress was one of a kind. It's still displayed in a glass frame at the Mercy Hill museum room in the public library.

Thank goodness Priscilla and Melody are on different floats today. Melody is riding with the other members of royalty, and Priscilla's on a float stuffed with the losers. Every year the royalty float goes at the end of the parade, but after the gown problem, Mrs. Reece insisted the winners go first. Momma says it's to make sure everybody sees Melody in that pink dress before they see Priscilla in hers. Melody's dress cost eighty-five dollars at the Great Gowns Emporium up in Louisville, but Priscilla's was just forty dollars at Donna's Dress Shop, where my momma works.

Momma thinks all this is funny, but she doesn't know how it is. All those popular girls will hate Priscilla for this. She'll have to do something to get back on their good sides. You just don't reduce Melody Reece to a regular person and get by with it.

I'm standing with Momma and Uncle Lu in front of the bandstand with the loudspeakers blaring in our ears and the Tiger Scouts running through the crowd like a bunch of hoodlums. I think about Jack and Lenny and Pop sitting in front of the hardware store in lawn chairs waiting for the parade. We could be there, too, if it weren't for Uncle Lucius wanting to hear the Shriners play their songs in the bandstand. So here we are, listening to a bunch of old men make the saxophones screech and the trumpets blast off-key, but Uncle Lu smiles and claps to the music, never hears a wrong note.

When the sirens start, the band stops playing. The police cars and fire trucks inch past us. Everybody waves. The firemen throw hard candy to the crowd. Peppermints left over from the Christmas parade. And the Mercy Hill Band marches by playing "The Stars and Stripes Forever!" Uncle Lu stands up straight with his hand over his heart.

The royalty float is all white. Carnations and crepe paper. You can't tell the real flowers from the fakes unless you're close to the float. The girls are sitting on white thrones waving to the crowd. Melody's smile looks like it's been painted on her face, like her mouth's smiling but her eyes are thinking about something else.

No one's noticing, anyway. The crowd's eyes are on the Tiny Miss, who can't sit still. With her bubbly yellow dress spread around her and the crown of fake flowers on her head she looks like a blossom that's slipped out of its pot. She wiggles and twists and clings to the side of her throne, getting as far away from the Tiny Mister as she can get. Everybody laughs. The Mister smiles and waves the way he's supposed to, but the Tiny Miss looks like she's about to cry.

On the heels of the royalty float the Shriners buzz by,

big men scrunched up in minicars wearing boxy hats with tassels.

A fancy black convertible car comes by with the mayor in the front seat and two strange men wearing suits in the back. A wide white banner taped to the side of the car says GIBSON-CARTER COAL COMPANY—MERCY HILL'S ROAD TO THE FUTURE. All the men are waving little American flags and smiling at the crowd.

"The road to destruction!" Uncle Lu calls out, but there's too much clapping for the men to hear.

Momma shakes her head at Uncle Lu.

"You're one hundred percent right about that, Lucius," Benny Moss says, edging his way through the crowd to stand beside Uncle Lu. "That bunch would be worse than the Matlocks."

Will Epperson taps his cane on the sidewalk to get people to move over and slips in beside the other two men. "We don't need strip miners in Mercy Hill," he says, holding up his cane and shaking it at the fancy convertible.

"What are they talking—"

"Watch the parade," Momma says.

The men in the black car keep smiling, waving their flags, and looking straight ahead.

And then comes the Reverend I. E. Fisher Jr., riding with the South Creek Baptist elders on a float with four pews and a huge wooden cross. The reverend

poses with his Bible open like he's ready to start a sermon any minute. One black pants leg has been cut up
the side to accommodate the cast he's been wearing
since he fell during the monkey sermon.

The "church on wheels" barely gets by before the Jellico Springs band comes dancing down the street, doing
a routine to "Locomotion." The trumpet players are
screeching on the high notes and the whole front row is
out of step.

"That's a snappy tune," Uncle Lu says. He doesn't
know the words, doesn't know it's rock and roll. Nobody
does. The preacher and the elders look back at the band and
smile, nod, thinking this is just another marching tune.

The loser float comes at the tail end of the parade. All
fake flowers and no thrones. The girls sit around the
edges dangling their legs over the sides like they're on a
fancy hayride. All the losers wave and smile except
Priscilla. She just sits there, her pink dress lost in the
rainbow around her.

People know when the show's over and start to fill the
street behind the last float. I see Willie Bright come pushing his way through the crowd and head toward us, and
Momma offers him a ride home.

"I thought Priscilla's dress was prettier than Melody's,"
he says.

"They're the exact same," I say. "Identical."

"But two dresses the same look different on different people," he says.

Sometimes I think Willie Bright's too smart for his own good.

 Confessing...

"Chileda!" Pop's voice is a round, cold stone thrown hard to hit its mark.

Twelve steps down the stairs, then the landing and four more. Maybe ten steps to the living room. I wish it were a million.

Pop's stretched out in the La-Z-Boy with his after-supper mug of Sanka, waiting for Walter Cronkite. The minute I look at him I know what's coming.

"Who broke the light shade?" He's pointing toward the ceiling but looking at me.

I can't lie. If Pop catches me in a lie, the punishment will be double. I could say Lenny did it and that would be a fact, but not the whole truth. Pop would keep digging until he got to the whole truth.

"We were having a show," I say. "Lenny and me."

"A show?" Pop frowns, looks up. "Who broke the light shade?"

"It was thin glass," I say. "It just fell apart."

Pop pushes in the footrest and sits straight up in the chair, his face red and his eyes wild. "WHO . . . BROKE . . ."

"Lenny hit it with Uncle Lu's walking stick."

Pop's face forms a puzzle. "Now, why would he do that?"

"He was dancing in—"

"LENNY!" Pop shouts so loud it hurts my ears.

That blue light shade cost fifty dollars at the antique fair. They don't make light shades like that anymore. A naked bulb hanging from a chain like that looks stupid. He wants to know—did we break it today? Yesterday?

"Last month," I say.

Pop chews on his lip like he's going to bite a hunk out of it.

"Get your money," he says, pointing to the stairs, where Lenny's now standing with his hands in his pockets. "And don't ever let me catch you dancing in this house again."

We rush upstairs and empty our banks. I have five dollars and eighty-five cents and Lenny has eight dollars and forty cents. I was going to buy a paperback at the Rexall on Saturday. Lenny had enough for the movies and a milkshake. We had plans.

We pool the coins—pennies, nickels, quarters—and

dump them in a brown paper bag. Not nearly enough to pay for the light shade.

When we get back downstairs, Pop's gone. The car's gone. Walter Cronkite's talking to himself in the living room.

"Sorry you can't dance anymore," I say to Lenny. I set the paper bag of money on the La-Z-Boy.

"I can't stop dancing," he says.

"You have to."

"We have to be more careful, that's all."

"You heard Pop."

"Nobody will know."

"You have to tell the truth," I say.

"Only if you're asked."

Lenny seems sure about this. The facts are one thing, the truth is another, and the whole truth is something else. And it's not entirely a lie to stay quiet if you're not asked.

I've been in bed awhile when I hear the back door slam. The metal stepladder opens with a loud squeak.

I slip out my bedroom door, stand at the railing, and listen. Pop's toolbox is open at the bottom of the stairs. He comes to the doorway and places the bare bulb and chain from the living-room ceiling onto the hallway rug and takes a plain white light shade from a cardboard box. The living room goes dark except for flashlight rays that shift and stop and shift again. Finally, the new light in place, the room explodes with the brightness of a hospital hallway. No more spotlight and shadows.

L*ures . . .*

I'm sitting at the kitchen table helping Uncle Lucius sort his fishing lures. Today he wants to use the bluish green ones only. No reds or orange or yellow. No solid colors. He's going after sunfish, he says, and they like the blue-greens.

"How do you know what they like?" I ask.

"You have to learn to think like a fish," he says.

He's brought two tackle boxes to the table and each one has a whole bunch of little compartments full of plastic lures and rubber worms. Some of the lures look like tiny fish with feathery tails and fins. The worms have segments on their bodies like real worms, except they're purple and pink and every other weird color you can imagine for a worm. I'm careful not to hook my fingers as I separate the blue-green lures and worms and line them up on the table.

The house is quiet. Everyone gone. I remember the

May Day parade, the mayor riding with those strange men, and Uncle Lu and his friends getting angry over that coal-company car being in the parade.

"What's strip-mining, Uncle Lu?"

"Scalping," he says, looking at me from across the table, his glasses sitting lopsided on his nose.

"Scalping?"

"They scrape away the trees and blast off the tops of the mountains."

"Why?"

"To get to the coal," he says. "It's cheap and easy that way."

"Are the strip miners coming to Mercy Hill?"

"Nope." He laughs and shakes his head. "They're just wishing and hoping."

"How do you—"

"The Mahoneys own this mountain," he says. "Your momma, that is."

"So . . ."

"Everything aboveground; everything below."

"Could we be rich if—"

"Doubtful," says Uncle Lu. "This land's not worth much except for the coal, and that mountain was not meant to be torn apart. It's been passed down through your momma's family."

I remember what Will Epperson said at the parade

and figure my uncle must have answers. "Why are the strip miners worse—"

"Look at this!" Uncle Lu holds up a set of keys and dangles them in front of me. The key ring has some kind of wooden whistle attached to it.

"What's that?"

"A duck call," he says. He puts the whistle to his lips and makes a strange sound like a hoarse bird trying to sing. "I used to hunt duck," he says. "But now I'm more *like* a duck."

"What do you mean?"

"I hunt fish." Uncle Lu laughs like this is the funniest joke anybody's ever told.

I hand him three pretty blue-green worms from my box that look almost like candy.

"Why are the strip miners worse than the Matlocks?" I ask, finally getting it all out.

"They bring destruction," he says. "They're all alike."

"Are these the same Matlocks as Miss Matlock who lives down the road?"

"They're all alike," he says again.

"But . . ."

Uncle Lu jumps up from the table and dangles those keys in my face again. "Now I know what these fit!" he says. "They're the keys to my boat."

"You don't have a boat anymore, Uncle Lu."

"It's red and white and it's hooked up down at the

river," he says. He turns and starts for the door. "We'll take out the boat. . . ."

"Aunt Gretchen sold it," I say. "Last summer. Remember?"

He comes back to the table with a puzzled look on his face, takes off his glasses, and sits back down across from me.

"I remember Gretchen," he says. "She was a pretty woman."

"But we were talking about the Matlocks. . . ."

He waves his hand to shush me. "I don't want to talk no more," he says.

Caught in the Wind...

Our water pump broke and the plumber says it'll take a week to get the part we need, so we go to Aunt Rose's house in town to get water. City water comes from the Cumberland River and Pop says it's nasty and tastes like chemicals. He'd take our well water any day, he says, even though it's full of iron and sulfur and turns the white clothes yellow.

Rose's wringer washing machine is sitting in the

middle of the kitchen floor taking up all the room. She washes and starches and irons shirts for the better men in town while their wives polish their nails and play cards.

We duck beneath a line of wet shirts and pants and boxy underwear to get to the sink. Momma and Jack fill their jugs first and Rose follows them to the front porch while they take their jugs to the car. I fill mine while Lenny waits in the doorway.

"That's the preacher's blue shirt," I say, pointing to the only blue amongst the whites and yellows.

"I think you're right," Lenny says.

"It's the one Zeno's little brother threw up on," I say, recalling how the preacher had picked up the baby and patted him on the back so hard his milk came up all over that blue shirt. It had small gray lines in it, almost invisible from a distance. "I'd like to put that shirt on a monkey."

Lenny laughs so hard he has to hold his belly. He'll laugh at anything I say.

I'm turned around watching him when Aunt Rose walks back in the kitchen.

"Look at that!" she shrieks, and points to the sink. "You know better than to waste water."

The faucet's on full blast and water is pouring over the jug. I turn it off, but Aunt Rose's face is aflame. She wipes off the counter even though it didn't really splash that far.

Lenny steadies his jug under the faucet.

"Is that the preacher's?" he asks, nodding toward the blue shirt.

"Well, yes, it is," Rose says. "How'd you know?"

"Zeno's little brother threw up on it," I say.

"What?" She examines the shirt for stains.

"You sure got it as clean as a whistle," Lenny says. He's grinning, probably still picturing a monkey in that starched blue shirt.

"I suppose I did," Rose says proudly.

Jack and Momma are waiting for us with the trunk open. I hand my water jugs to Jack and slip into the backseat beside Lenny. When we get ready to go, Aunt Rose leans in through Jack's open window.

"You all ought to stay awhile," she says. "You can go home when you can't go no place else."

We're all still laughing when Momma turns the key and pulls out into the going-down sun.

You can always go home. Your true home stays put. It's all those other places in the outside world that you can't always go to, maybe never go to, except in dreams. These mountains keep a firm hold. I once read about an earthquake on the other side of the world and that night I dreamt the mountains moved. The river and the meadow and the woods got smaller and smaller as the mountains closed in and squeezed out all the air.

Sometimes when a storm whips through this valley on its way to someplace else, I feel trapped, caught in the wind.

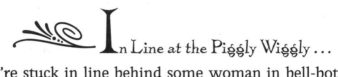In Line at the Piggly Wiggly...

We're stuck in line behind some woman in bell-bottom jeans and a rabbit-fur vest. It's way too hot for a vest like that.

She takes her time emptying the cart, talking to Rusty Peters behind the counter.

Aunt Rose turns around and rolls her eyes at me. "That one's bound to be a VISTA," she whispers.

I look down at my feet, hoping the rabbit woman doesn't hear.

Rose shakes her head. "The only time they come here to trade is when the A&P over in Jellico Springs runs out of something," she says.

The rabbit woman turns around, but she looks past us and scans the aisles. People are always getting halfway checked out and then remembering something else they need. She bends over the counter and says something to

Rusty, but I can't hear because of all the adding-machine noise.

Rusty stops tapping keys and goes up on his toes so his head's above the stack of cornflakes on sale at the checkout.

"Hey, Jimmy!" he shouts to Jimmy Dupree, the produce boy. "Where's the *falafel* mix at?"

Dead silence. Heads in line at the two other checkout counters turn and look our way. Somebody says: "*Awful* mix?"

"Aisle three," a voice calls from somewhere between the oranges and cabbage.

The rabbit/VISTA woman squeezes past Aunt Rose and me and hurries down aisle three like she's headed to a fire.

"What on earth is that?" Rose asks.

Rusty smiles and shakes his head. "She had us special-order it," he says. "It's probably foreign."

"That's what I was thinking," says Rose. She scoots our hot rolls and tea bags and buttermilk down the counter so she has enough room for the bleach and the Ajax. Rose is planning to clean and cook today while Momma's at work. She's tired of looking at the tea stains on our sink, she says. We're too sloppy. Rose couldn't stand to live with us for one minute. She'd go crazy, she says. Still, she's at our house almost as much as I am.

We wait in line, listen to Roger Miller singing in the

background. *I've been a long time leaving, yeah, but I'll be a long time gone.* . . . I look down aisle two and spot the cassette player stuck on the top shelf beside the Tide laundry detergent.

When the rabbit lady comes back, I look at the box in her hand and memorize the spelling so I can add it to my list. *Falafel.* On one side of the box there's a picture of a man in white pants gathering some kind of grass in a big field.

Rusty's fingers dance across the keys on the adding machine like he's playing a piano while the rabbit lady loads up her own bags. She pays with cash and leaves. Through the big picture windows we can see her put the grocery bags into a blue jeep that's covered with mud, like it's been up and down every hollow in the county.

"What's Mercy Hill coming to?" Rose says, clicking her tongue.

"Beats me," says Rusty.

Jimmy Dupree comes up and leans over the partition behind Rusty.

"We had to order a dozen boxes of that *falafel* stuff," he says. "The main company wouldn't let us buy just one."

"That's a dirty shame," says Rose.

"We need more people to buy it," Jimmy says.

"Don't look at me," says Rose.

They all laugh like this is some kind of joke.

We do not eat weird food in Mercy Hill. Last month

Momma bought a *Ladies' Home Journal* magazine so she could try a recipe for Polynesian pork, but she had to throw away most of the pork because nobody liked it except Lenny and me. It had pineapple in it. "Who puts pineapple in stew?" Pop said. "It's a waste of money to cook food that nobody eats." So mostly we eat fried chicken or meat loaf, mashed potatoes, and green beans out of the garden, and everybody's happy. Uncle Lu says magazine recipes are for city people anyway, people who can't cook.

Sometimes I see Momma reading the recipes in magazines at the Piggly Wiggly store, but she just looks now. Buying magazines is a waste of money, too.

Going to Mexico...

Miss Matlock brings a bag of plastic cars to school. Blue four-door sedans for the boys and pink convertibles for the girls. The boys would be jealous of the convertibles except none of them would drive a pink car.

She has us put our chairs in a big circle like we used to do in kindergarten.

"Story time!" Zeno Mayfield says this loud enough

for everyone to hear, but Miss Matlock doesn't even look at him.

"Put the library table in the middle," she says, pointing to the long work table back near the lockers. The boys carry it to the center of the room. Zeno pulls up his shirt sleeve and flexes his make-believe muscles.

"Are we having a race?" a bunch of voices cry at once. They roll cars across the desks and make zooming sounds.

We're way too old for this.

Miss Matlock unrolls a map of Canada, the United States, and Mexico and tapes it to the tabletop. She circles the spot in Kentucky where Mercy Hill is and takes a kitchen timer from her desk.

"Who wants to be first?"

All the boys jump up, but Zeno gets to the table first. Is that any surprise?

"Start here in Kentucky," Miss Matlock says. She has him close his eyes and tilt his head toward the ceiling so there's absolutely no cheating. "Drive until the timer dings."

Half a breath after *Go*, Zeno's car is sitting in the Pacific Ocean. Miss Matlock draws a little *x* on the spot and writes his name.

All the boys *zoom* their cars across the country, but no one else gets to the Pacific. Two cars end up in Canada, but the rest stop in states across the West. The girls drive slower. Since we don't know what kind of game we're playing, it's best to be cautious.

"We're going to Mexico," Miss Matlock says when we're all done and every spot has been marked with an *x*. The boys in California and Arizona and Texas are excited. They're almost there already. Willie Bright is sitting in Laredo, right on the border, even though he didn't try to zip across the states like the others. He just headed in the right direction.

"Willie knew where we were going," Ginny says. "He had to know."

"I didn't know," says Willie.

Miss Matlock says: "This is not a race."

Ginny whispers to Priscilla: "A welfare wouldn't have enough gas money to get to Texas." The two of them giggle and everybody wants to know what they're laughing about.

"Enough nonsense," says Miss Matlock. She explains the project. We each have to do a short report about the state we landed on—the historic places, the weather and crops and customs, what the land looks like. Are there mountains? Or prairie? Or wilderness? And how about lakes, rivers, or deserts? What do the people do for work? The boys who've made the most progress cross-country will also have to write one extra paragraph about each of the states they have driven across to get where they are sitting. They all groan. It's not fair, they say. The girls have it easy.

"But everyone must end up in Mexico," Miss Matlock says. The next time we can each choose where we stop so long as we get to Mexico in two weeks. "We'll arrive together," she says.

"That's not a race," says Zeno.

"Exactly," says Miss Matlock. "This is not a race."

"What am I supposed to do?" Zeno asks. "I'm floatin' in the ocean."

"Tell us about the Pacific," Miss Matlock says. "And, of course, a little something about all those states you drove so fast through to get to the ocean."

"What if I didn't drive?" Zeno asks. "What if I flew in an airplane? I could be in Mexico in a minute."

Everybody laughs.

"Hardly a minute," Miss Matlock says. "And we're all driving." She takes Zeno's blue car and places it on the coast of California. "Let's say you stopped in Los Angeles. There is much to see and do and *write* about while you wait for the others to get across the country."

Zeno grabs the blue car from Miss Matlock, but she doesn't scold him. Just raises her eyebrows, looks over her glasses.

After class, everyone pours into the hallway, and soon there's a huddle and they're all complaining about Miss Matlock and the stupid assignments and how this is supposed to be English class and we haven't opened our grammar books since she came to teach.

"We're writing papers," I say. "That's grammar."

"Why do you always take up for her?" Ginny asks.

"You and that Willie Bright Eyes," Zeno says. "The two of you knew about this project, didn't you? Chili and Willie in a conspiracy with the old crazy lady."

When the bell rings, we have to run to get to the next class. Obviously, Zeno didn't notice that I landed in northern Indiana. I would be closer to Mexico if I'd stayed in Mercy Hill, Kentucky.

Offerings 1 . . .

Sunday morning. We fill up a whole pew since Pop talked Myra and Uncle Lu into coming to church.

Two strange men and a woman walk in and sit across the aisle from us where the Murphys usually sit, and the Murphys have to take the next row and push everybody else back. Ginny's mother is not pleased. You can tell by the look on her face.

The men are wearing T-shirts and the woman has on

black pants. Around here women don't wear pants to
church. Everybody stares and whispers.

"VISTAs," Momma says. "They have to be VISTAs."

The man sitting at the end of the pew pats his foot
when the organ starts playing. Up front Pop stands to
sing his solo, the first verse of "Whispering Hope."

> *Soft as the voice of an angel, breathing*
> *a lesson unheard . . .*

Sunlight falls in streaks of color through the stained-
glass window.

On the last two verses everybody stands and sings,
even the VISTAs. But they don't know the words and
have to look at the songbook.

When it's time for the orphans' offering, Jack puts in
his quarter and passes the plate to me and Lenny and we
drop in ours. Pop gives each of us two dollars a week to
spend, but we have to save a quarter of it for the Jellico
Springs Orphans' Home.

I see one of the VISTA men fold up a check and drop it
in the plate.

"The preacher prefers real money," Aunt Rose whispers to Momma. "Checks can bounce."

"I doubt they'd do something like that in a church,"
I say.

"Hmph . . . ," Rose says. "You'd be surprised what some people will do."

"Maybe they gave more money than you did, Aunt Rose."

"I'm certain that's not—"

"But what if they did? What if that check was for a hundred dollars?"

"I always give my fair share," Rose says. "Ten percent of every penny I make ends up in this church house."

"Ten percent?"

"That's right," she says. "That's what's required."

After church the three strangers shake hands with the preacher and head for the parking lot.

"I guess some people are too busy for a cup of coffee," Frances Perkins says.

We all go to the church basement for coffee and homemade jelly rolls, and there is much discussion about the way the VISTA people were dressed and whether or not that check will bounce. Finally, the preacher says to stop and everybody stops talking about the strangers. Like switching radio stations, they start talking about the jelly rolls, making it sound like they're the most exotic pastries in the world, even though Miss Perkins has been making these same rolls on the last Sunday of every month for years.

When it's time to leave, we can't find Uncle Lu. We

go different directions, Jack and me and Lenny, up and down the church-house stairs, in and out of the bathrooms. Finally, Pop spots him sitting in the car.

All the way home Uncle Lu talks about the orphans in Jellico Springs. He'd raise them all if he could, he says, because he was never blessed with children. I imagine his tiny house on Sycamore Street filled with kids hanging out the windows.

At home Momma and Aunt Rose peel potatoes and flour chicken and mash egg yolks for a dozen deviled eggs. When we all sit down to eat, I can't help wondering how much money it would take to feed a bunch of kids. I remember something Aunt Rose said.

"The required church offering is only ten percent," I say.

"That's right," says Rose. "And I give every penny of it."

"But why do *we* have to give a quarter?" I ask, looking over at Pop. "Ten percent of two dollars . . ."

Pop puts down his fork, stands up, and points his finger at me and Lenny.

"The two of you ought to be ashamed." Pop's face is red and his top lip is quivering.

I want to tell him that I didn't really mean to take money away from the orphans and Lenny didn't even know I was going to say it. It was just a simple question.

fferings 2 . . .

Momma and Aunt Rose are sitting at the kitchen table listening to the *Sunday Gospel Sing* on the radio. I get on my bike and head up Persimmon Tree Road, feeling ashamed about the orphans one minute and as free as a fox the next. The world is full of good and bad feelings that go on at the same time.

When I drop my bike and start down the path through the woods, I run into Willie Bright, his yellow hair flamed with sunlight.

"Where you going?" he asks.

Should I tell him? I guess he's not the sort to blab.

"Miss Matlock's house," I say.

"Have you seen all those books of hers? Some of those foreign people are a lot poorer than we are," he says.

It must make Willie Bright feel good to hear about people who are worse off than he is.

"When did *you* start going to her house?" I ask.

"The day she moved back here," he says. "How about you?"

I shrug and look away. "A long time ago," I say. "I forget exactly." I don't tell Willie that I didn't even meet Miss Matlock until she became our teacher. I'd seen her puttering in the garden but never stopped to talk. There were all those rumors. . . .

"I'd get in trouble for sure if my grandma ever found out about me coming here," Willie says.

So he's not supposed to go to Miss Matlock's house either. I wonder if he knows something I don't know.

"Why is that?" I ask.

"Granny says Miss Matlock's nuts and she's mean, too."

"I like her," I say.

"Well, she's been a lot of places," he says. "Miss Matlock's seen the world."

"I know," I say. "I'm going to be just like her and leave here someday, too."

"I'll go with you," Willie Bright offers.

"What?" I study this boy's shiny face for a minute and know he means it. "Not with *me*," I say. "I'm not taking anybody."

We start up the hill to the house and he reaches into his pocket and pulls out a red feather.

"It's from a cardinal bird," he says. He found it under the willow trees.

I bend over to look at the feather and run upon Willie Bright's lopsided smile. It's like a pause on the television. The picture freezes. It doesn't move again until he sticks the feather in my hair.

Sign-up Day . . .

Every class has three groups—the As, Double As, and Triple As—slow, average, and fast. It used to be As, Bs, and Cs until somebody complained that it wasn't right. It was like saying that one group was automatically going to get Cs. They usually did.

I'm in the Double As, and we get mostly Bs. That's the best place to be if you don't want to work too hard or be called a nerd or a brain or stupid.

But our three groups won't be together next year. In eighth grade we get put in separate classes. Most of the average students, the Double As, sign up for general classes—general math, general science, basic English; advanced students take the honors courses—pre-algebra, pre-biology, all the hard stuff. The slow ones get put in general classes with special-education teachers so they can learn how to study and get organized before they tackle high school.

The tests we took help the counselor figure out where we ought to be next year, but we don't have to do what she says. There are no rules. If you're an average student, you can still choose to take the advanced classes if you want to work like a dog and barely pass.

At lunchtime Ginny stops at each of the Double As' tables.

"All the cool kids are signing up for general classes," she says, bending over my chair. "Boys don't like girls who are nerds or dummies."

Since I don't have any friends in the other groups anyway, there's no question about which way to go.

After school Miss Matlock asks if I signed up for the advanced classes.

"No," I say. "Why would I—"

"You're just marking time," she says.

"Marking time?"

"You're not going anyplace." She looks at Willie and shakes her head. "You too," she says. "You both need a challenge."

"I can't do the work," Willie says.

"Don't ever say *can't*," Miss Matlock says. "*Can't* never accomplished anything."

"But I—"

"Get somebody to help you," she says. She looks over at me and raises her eyebrows.

"I make Bs," I say. "I'm no tutor. Besides . . ." I can't think of a besides.

Maybe Miss Matlock *is* a little crazy. Willie Bright would flunk out of school if he took the advanced courses. Everybody knows that. And I'd make Cs and Pop would have a fit and ground me for the school year. And if I helped Willie get out of the dummy group, nobody in the former Double As would speak to me again. Miss Matlock doesn't understand how life works around here. Maybe she was gone too long.

Old Tate and Foxy Lady . . .

Aunt Rose smears sulfur salve on Old Tate. He's a brown-and-white-spotted bird dog, but right now he's mostly pink-skinned with the mange. It makes him scratch and whine and turn in fierce circles when the itching starts, so Aunt Rose made a batch of her lard-and-sulfur mange cure.

"Don't hurt him!" I yell at Rose. She clamps down on

Old Tate's collar and slaps the salve all over his body with a wooden paint stick while he whimpers and twists and tries to get loose. Foxy Lady's tied to the cherry tree, with her tail between her legs and her head down. She knows she's next in line.

Aunt Rose drops a blob of salve in Tate's food bowl and he laps it up like Purina. The only way to kill the mange is to work at it from the inside, too, she says. But when Rose tries to drag Foxy Lady to the sulfur pot, the dog gets loose and runs away.

I take off around the house after her and see Lenny sitting on the porch swing reading a book.

"Where'd Foxy go?" I ask, figuring he must have seen something.

He shakes his head. "Wasn't watching," he says.

The front yard is as quiet as a graveyard. Every now and then you can hear a dove cooing.

Rose comes around the corner of the house with her face red and her curly hair wet with sweat. "Wait till I get my hands on that dog," she says.

"She's gone," I say. "Foxy's gone." I plop down on the porch swing next to Lenny and he gives it a shove, making the chains squeak.

Rose throws up her hands and heads back around the house. When Lenny stops the swing, I can hear short breaths between the dove coos. Frantic at first, it slows to a soft, even rhythm. Foxy Lady is asleep under the wooden porch.

Lenny looks over at me and smiles. He turns to a glossy page in his book with a picture of the ocean. It's the prettiest blue I've ever seen. Turquoise.

"Do you think the ocean is really that color?" I ask.

"Yep," says Lenny. "I'd say so."

"Someday I'm going to the real ocean."

"We'll go together," he says.

"Nope. I'm going by myself."

Lenny shrugs and gives the swing another push. I don't want to hurt his feelings, but when I picture myself leaving Mercy Hill, I'm always traveling alone. Not with Lenny and not with Willie Bright.

After Rose goes home, I hold Foxy on my lap and stroke her ears while Lenny paints her with sulfur salve. When I leave Mercy Hill, I might just take a dog with me.

Flying . . .

We're babysitting Ginny's little brother, Clayburne, and he says: "Let's fly to Neverland."

We take off our shoes and crawl inside the cardboard box the Murphys' new refrigerator came in. You wouldn't have to take off your shoes and crawl into a real airplane.

Ginny's behind me with Clayburne on her lap and Priscilla is all the way in the back, leaning against the box and making it move from side to side.

"We're experiencing turbulence," I say, talking into my fist like it's a microphone.

"What?" Both girls speak at once.

"Turbulence. Lenny says that's what it's called when an airplane ride is bumpy."

"Like potholes in the road?" Priscilla asks.

"I guess."

"How would Lenny know?" Ginny says. "He's never been on an airplane."

"Lenny knows," I say.

I look out the round window we've cut in the cardboard airplane and catch sight of a real jet passing in and out of the clouds. I wonder what Mercy Hill looks like to all those outsiders. Would it look the same to me from up there as it does to a person who's never gotten any closer to us than the clouds? I'll bet you could see right past these mountains. They couldn't hold you back.

Miss Matlock's world globe doesn't have a single

speck on it to show that Mercy Hill exists. Still, you can feel the Appalachians. They're like a row of pimples down the slick face of America. But you can't see or feel the rivers that twist through the green valleys, or the way the willow trees bend over and dip their branches in the water, or the crawdads that hide in mud castles along the banks.

Sometimes I twirl the globe and stop to see where my finger lands, pretending I'll go there someday, but most of the time I land smack in the middle of the ocean on the other side of the world.

Priscilla's pushing hard now, making the box sway from side to side. At some point she'll lean too far and we'll start rolling across the yard and keep rolling until we get dizzy and have to stop. Clayburne will probably get hurt and start crying and tell on us. That's how it usually goes. "You're too big to play in boxes," they'll say. "That's not what babysitting is all about."

I look up and watch the real airplane disappear into the sun, leaving nothing but its white streaks across the sky. That's what I want to do. I want to ride in a silver plane someday and leave my own white streaks high above Mercy Hill.

Willie's Granny Dies...

Willie Bright is standing at the bus stop in the sprinkling rain. He's not even wearing a jacket. He looks at me with red eyes.

"Granny died," he says.

I don't know what to say. He never once mentioned that the old woman was sick, only that she was mean. Too mean to die, he once said. Maybe he regrets it now.

"I'm sorry," I say. I guess I'm sorry. I didn't really know her that well, don't know how to feel, don't know what he's expecting.

"It's okay," he says. "She was old." He turns to walk away. "I won't be going to school," he says.

I start to offer to take his homework in or tell the teachers, but the rain starts coming down harder and I pull up my hood and slip my books under my jacket to keep them from getting wet. When I look up, he's gone.

Third period Miss Matlock sits at her desk with her hands in her lap waiting for the bell. Everybody's talking. Zeno has brought in his baseball-card collection and is passing the cards around, trying to get some of the boys to swap because he has a lot of duplicates.

When Miss Matlock coughs, everybody gets quiet.

"Helena Wilkins died last night," she says.

Helena.

"Who's that?" Ginny asks.

"Willie's grandmother," Miss Matlock says.

Tomorrow she'll send flowers from the third-period English class if we all bring in a little extra money. Helena was once a friend, she says. They were girls together.

"A friend?" Ginny and Priscilla frown at each other.

"Normal teachers aren't *friends* with welfares," Ginny whispers across the aisle.

If they were once friends, why weren't they friends now? Why wouldn't Willie's grandma want him going to Miss Matlock's house? Not questions to ask in school, I suppose.

The day flies by and Willie's grandmother is not mentioned again. I guess none of the other teachers knew her. Maybe they're all too young.

At the dinner table Momma says she'll go to the funeral. It'll be at the Osborne Funeral Home, she says. They couldn't possibly set the old woman up for a viewing at the Bright house.

"Her name was Helena," I say.

Six heads turn toward me.

"That's right," says Pop.

Momma stirs cream into her coffee. "It's a shame they have to bury her in the pauper's lot."

"She was friends with Miss Matlock when they were girls," I say. "That's what Miss Matlock told us today."

Pop clears his throat like he's got something stuck in it. "Helena Wilkins was a maid," he says. "She worked for the Matlocks. Not exactly a friend, I'd say."

"A maid?" I didn't know anybody in Mercy Hill had ever had a maid. "But Miss Matlock said—"

"You can't believe half what people tell you," Pop says. "You have to watch what they do."

"What does that mean?"

"Just what I said. Sometimes the mouth says one thing and the heart does something else."

"Still, they were girls together," I say. "Like Ginny and Priscilla and me."

Pop laughs again. "I can't imagine any other peas in a pod like the three of you."

At bedtime I think about what Pop said, about the mouth saying one thing and the heart doing another.

Third period Miss Matlock tells us she's bought a basket of white lilies for Willie's grandmother with the collection of leftover lunch money, and she asks us all to sign the card. Everyone writes *I'm sorry.* When the card lands on my desk, I sit thinking until my pencil is wet with sweat. I try to come up with a verse or a pretty saying or something Miss Matlock has read to us or even a word from my word list that would just fit, but my mind is empty. I write: *I'm sorry.* Under it I sign my full name, Chileda Sue Mahoney, like that makes a difference.

 Winding Down...

The days fly by, and the pink and white flowers of wild redbuds and dogwoods blow away with the wind, leaving the new leaves of spring to darken and turn the hillsides a deep, rich green. At night a zillion lightning bugs zip and dive above the timothy grass in the meadow. During the day, when the fireflies sleep, the hay grass is full of yellow sulfur butterflies and tiny loopers.

Two more days until we're free. School's winding down and summer's winding up. My favorite time. Jack's and Lenny's, too. Every kid in Mercy Hill is wearing a smile.

At suppertime Pop says everybody has to "get his ducks in a row." Get organized for the summer. He says we can't just sit around doing nothing. Lenny and Jack will help Pop out at the hardware store when Jack's not at summer football practice and Lenny's not at the library. Lenny has a whole list of books he has to get through this summer because he signed up for the advanced classes next fall.

Everybody has to do garden work, and you can't do much planning for it because you never know when it will rain or the sun will shine, when there'll be weeds to pull up or sprouts to water. It's like being "on call," Pop says.

"What are *your* plans, Chili?" Pop looks at me as if I'm supposed to have plans, but I was counting on being free as a bird, just like I've been every other summer.

"What do you mean?"

"You're almost thirteen," he says. "Time to think about what you want to get done this summer."

I have to think fast. "Books," I say. "I think I might read a lot."

Pop raises his eyebrows and stares at me for a long time, maybe five seconds. "It's okay to read," he says, "if you're aiming in some direction. But don't waste time on foolishness."

"Foolishness?"

"On nonsense," he says. "Don't hole up in this house reading books from the Rexall and turning peaked when you could be out in the fresh air."

"I can read outside," I say. "Besides, the fresh air around here is full of cow manure."

Lenny and Jack start everybody laughing. Everybody except Pop, and he just looks at me and shakes his head.

"You heard me," he says.

I nod and go back to eating my shuck beans, the last of the dried beans from the cellar.

"Next time we have green beans, they'll be fresh off the vine," Momma says in her best bird-chirping, change-the-subject voice.

Workers...

The back of Miss Matlock's little green truck is loaded with tools—a pick, a long-handled shovel, a mattock, a hoe, and hedge clippers.

"Get in," she says. "We've got work to do."

"Work?" I say.

"Work?" Willie says.

It's the first day of summer vacation. Work is the last thing I want to do.

Miss Matlock had promised to show Willie and me pictures of Italy and make a special dessert. *Cannoli.* Crisp and creamy, she called it. But when we got to the house, she said it would have to wait; there was an important project to get started. She didn't say one thing about us driving anywhere. Pop would ground me for life if he knew I was getting in this truck.

She turns the key and the old engine coughs and sputters twice before hitting on a running rhythm.

"I'm not supposed to leave Persimmon Tree Road," I say. "If anybody sees us, I'll get in trouble."

"Not going to pass anybody," Miss Matlock says. "We're going up on the mountain."

"Why?"

"To do something that ought to have been done years ago."

Willie looks at me and I shrug.

"What?" he asks.

"You'll see."

At the Mercy Hill cemetery the pavement ends. The road up the mountain is all dirt and rocks and cinders. It used to be a coal road and big trucks rolled down the mountain carrying their loads from the mine, but the mine's been shut down for years. In the winter, though, we can still fill buckets with enough coal for the fireplace.

The cemetery looks like a big grassy lawn with gray and black and pink shiny headstones to mark the graves. Two of the tombs are made from a stone that's almost white. Some of the small stones have lambs carved on the top, some have crosses, some are flying tiny American flags. A few of the graves are covered with plastic flowers that can last for months and still look good, and the whole cemetery is surrounded by a chain-link fence with orange trumpet vines twisting through the metal.

Miss Matlock stops the truck where the fence stops. This is the pauper's lot. The poor people are buried outside the fence in the musk thistle and weeds and wild blackberry briars. There are no stones, just little metal markers with the names written on a slip of paper covered with plastic. Some of the papers are blank, the names long washed away by the rains. Willie points to his granny's grave, a cleared spot covered with clay dirt and a few droopy white lilies.

"We'll make it bloom," Miss Matlock says.

I can't imagine how. The pauper's lot is never cleaned or mowed or planted like the real cemetery. I remember coming up here on Decoration Day. I had helped Momma and Aunt Rose make crepe-paper flowers—yellow mums, red roses, and pink and white tulips. We worked for a week twisting the petals and leaves into place on wires and covering the stems in green before dipping them in hot wax so they'd hold up against the rains. The women lined up behind the tombstones to take pictures that day, and all around them the cemetery bloomed like a fancy garden.

But I've never seen anyone decorate the pauper's lot. I'm thinking we're probably not supposed to be doing this. There might even be a law against it.

"What if we get in trouble?" I ask.

"What if, what if, what if," Miss Matlock says, like I'm talking nonsense. She reaches over the side of the truck and takes out the clippers. "I'll clip the briars back and you two dig up the roots."

We were supposed to walk through the catacombs today, to stand in the Roman Forum and the Coliseum. I grab the hoe and start whacking hard at the chigger weeds.

"No! No!" Miss Matlock yells. "Leave those flowers."

"But they're chigger weeds. We'll get a million bites."

"That's Queen Anne's lace," she says. "It makes a pretty border."

Momma always chops down the chigger-weed "borders" at the edge of our garden. Bug bites are no fun. How will I explain getting eaten alive?

Willie Bright digs up blackberry-briar roots and we take them to the woods with the clumps of crabgrass and cockleburs. With each trip we have to pick burs off our shirts and shorts. I check his back and he checks mine.

"We'll do a little at a time," Miss Matlock says. She wants us to go over every inch of the pauper's lot until it's rid of weeds and briars so we can plant flowers. Flowers that will come back on their own every year, she says, so it won't matter that people don't bring baskets to decorate these graves. She's going to buy purple sage and pincushion flowers. Dragon's blood and dusty miller. Goldenrod and red-hot pokers to line the fence that separates this from the real cemetery.

We've barely cleared half the lot when a mass of dark clouds rolls in without warning and it starts pouring. We run for the truck.

Finally, we're bouncing back down the mountain and onto the slippery pavement. I cross my fingers that nobody sees us, that I don't have chiggers running loose in my clothes, and that I get home before Momma does.

After we help Miss Matlock put away the garden tools, I take off down Persimmon Tree Road with Willie trailing behind me. The sun's back, breaking through the clouds, and everything that was soaked has started steaming. The dark trunks of the maples, the rocks and pebbles and dirt along the roadway, the hot pavement.

Everything giving off steam like a big cooking pot, setting the water free to go back up in the clouds.

"Rain wraiths," Willie Bright says, catching up to me.

"What on earth are you talking about?"

"That's what Granny used to call the road fog. Rain wraiths."

"Do you even know what a wraith is?" The minute I ask I want to bite my tongue. He probably doesn't know and I'm sure I don't know and now he'll expect me to explain.

"Ghosts," he says. "Wraiths are like ghosts."

"What kind of ghosts?"

"People ghosts, maybe."

"Under this pavement?"

"People ghosts from a thousand years ago, maybe," he says. "When there were no roads."

"It's steam, Willie. Plain old water going back up to the clouds."

"I know that."

"Then why—"

"It's just what my granny said. Sometimes I like to pretend."

"Pretend there are ghosts flying up from the highway?" I shake my head. This boy has some strange thoughts. He's the last person I'd expect to pretend. He never even believed in Santa Claus.

"You can pretend about anything," he says. "Anything at all."

"Well," I say, "if these were ghosts, they'd be the
ghosts of ants and grasshoppers and road kill, because
that's all you'll find here."

We walk in silence. A bird starts singing a long way
off in the woods. Our shoes slap against the hot, wet
pavement. I look over and see Willie Bright walking
with his eyes closed, smiling, taking in deep breaths full
of ghosts.

 The Lives of Eels...

"I wish we were sitting on a rock in the Sargasso Sea,"
Miss Matlock says. "At least, we'd have the trade winds
blowing through our hair."

We're drinking lemonade at the dining-room table.
It's ninety-five degrees; too hot for tea.

"Where's the Sargasso Sea?" I ask.

"Bring me the globe," she says.

I go to the parlor and bring back the world globe. She
spins it slowly and puts down her finger in the middle of

the ocean east of Florida and north of the long band of Caribbean islands.

"That's the Atlantic Ocean," I say.

"Ah, yes," she says, "but this part is also the Sargasso Sea." She makes a circle with her finger, says it's the only sea in the world that has no shores, a sea of calm in the middle of fierce currents. "It's separate from the Atlantic."

"How?" I ask. To me the blues all run together and look the same.

"This area is very salty," she explains, "and sometimes there's no wind at all." She tells me the water in this spot was once believed to be lifeless, but it's actually full of floating sargassum seaweed and millions of eels. "Eels are born here," she says, "and they die here, too."

"How long do eels live?"

"Twenty years. Maybe thirty. I'd have to look it up."

"Thirty years circling one spot when there's a whole ocean to see?"

"No, no, no," she says. "They spend all those in-between years in faraway places." When an eel hatches, it's not really an eel, she tells me; it's a tiny transparent fish. Currents carry the larvae toward North America, but a mysterious force causes them to separate so that some drift to Europe. And then they are all transformed.

"Transformed?"

"This is when they change from fish to eel," she says, "and the males and females separate, too." The males stay in the harbors, but the females swim upstream to creeks and rivers. She says a girl eel might swim from the Gulf of Mexico all the way to Minnesota.

"But how can they live out of the salt water?" I don't know anything about the Sargasso Sea, but I do know that saltwater fish can't live in the Cumberland River.

"Some mystery of nature helps them adapt," she says. The females can live in a pond or lake or river in Kansas or Nebraska or even some little village in France for ten or twenty years, she tells me. But then they make a final journey. They eat as much as they can, the way a caterpillar eats before it becomes a butterfly, and head back across the ocean with their bodies changing as they go so that they can live in salt water again. At the coasts they join up with the male eels and head back to the Sargasso Sea.

"That's a long way to swim," I say. "How do they find their way back?"

"No one knows," she says. "But they always do."

Miss Matlock says that the eels lay their eggs and eventually die, that nothing but death could stop them from taking that journey across the sea, and nothing but death could keep them from coming back home again.

Myra's Poems...

Myra keeps a diary. She writes in it every night, but she won't let me read it. She says she's making notes about the baby.

Before Myra met Jerry Wilson and got her life ruined, she was planning to go to college. But the day after high school graduation they ran off to North Carolina and got married. Momma still cries when Myra tells about putting on her green prom dress at a Shell station off Interstate 75.

Some nights when Myra is writing at her desk, Momma stands in the doorway and smiles. Maybe she pretends Myra is still home doing her lessons and Jerry Wilson never existed, but then she looks over at me and gets jolted back to the right time. If I'm twelve, Myra can't possibly be doing her high school homework. When I smile at Momma, she turns and walks out of the room.

This morning Momma and Myra are going over to

Jellico Springs to have lunch at the Bird's Nest Restaurant, a spiffy place with real tablecloths on the Formica tables. They serve club sandwiches at lunchtime just like the fine restaurants in the city. Momma's favorite is the ham-and-cheese club on white toast. She makes me hungry just talking about it, but she doesn't ask me to go. She and Myra have *issues* to discuss.

After they leave, I run upstairs and watch the car turn onto Persimmon Tree Road, climb the hill toward town, and disappear. I picture the two of them sailing down the interstate highway. Momma and Myra and the baby-to-be on their way to a ham-and-cheese sandwich, while I'm left with chicken noodle soup and peanut butter with crackers because no one remembered to buy bread.

I slip Myra's diary from the desk drawer and sit by the window so I can watch the road in case they forgot something and decide to come back. I skip around from one page to another but don't find a single word about the baby. Every page has a verse and most of the verses talk about a man, but there's a space with little stars where the name ought to be. She writes about hearing his footsteps on the wooden porch, but Myra has a concrete porch at her house in Jellico Springs. He plays the piano, she writes, and splays pages of music across the floor.

I look up *splays* and read on through a string of

words I've never heard . . . *adagio, sonatina, pizzicato, concerto, andante, arpeggio.* I pull my red notebook from my backpack and add these to my word list, making two observations: Jerry Wilson never laid hands on a piano, and these words sound like they were written by someone I've never met. Still, they are full of Myra's sadness.

Women in the Park . . .

After dinner we sit in the front yard breaking beans. The garden rows are thick now with Cherokee yellows, purple snaps, Jacob's Cattle bush beans, and Kentucky Wonders. Green, yellow, purple, and speckled. We strip away the strings and break each bean into sections for canning.

The Murphys drive by in their green Chevrolet and beep the horn to let us know they're headed to the park. Ginny and Priscilla wave from the backseat.

"We need a break from this," Momma says. She dumps the bean strings and ends from her apron into an empty bushel basket and goes to the house to get her pocketbook while I put on my sandals and Pop starts the station wagon.

Rose stands up to dust off her dress and calls after Momma. "Tell Myra to come with us tonight," she says.

Myra won't come. She hates to go to the park because of the bugs and all the questions from the women. She hasn't talked much since she and Momma went to Jellico Springs and discovered a lot of Jerry Wilson's clothes missing. There's no way he could have been wearing all those clothes when he drowned. And, if he knew ahead of time that he was going to drown himself, why did he take a bunch of clothes? Questions whirl in the air and never land on the answers.

I see Myra standing at the bedroom window watching us leave. She's too big for regular clothes, so Aunt Rose, who is plenty overweight, gave Myra some of her big flowered tops and muumuu dresses, which fit perfectly. She looks like a walking flowerpot.

At the park the men choose partners for horseshoes and go off to play under the floodlights. In the speckled tree shadows the women talk about the good old days. There's Momma, Mary Martin, Aunt Rose, Edna Murphy, Mrs. Nelson, and the Tubbs girls. The Tubbs girls are twins, never married. Momma says one can't do anything without the other and no man would put up with that.

We sit with the women, listening to stories about the good old days until I'm bored to the point of misery.

"Let's go to the bandstand," I say.

The bandstand sits on stilts like a giant tree house,

and the bushes around it are full of lightning bugs flickering like tiny Christmas lights.

"When's Myra going to have that baby?" Ginny asks.

I shrug. "Not sure."

"How can you not know something like that?"

I catch a lightning bug and let it crawl up my arm. "Do you know why these bugs light up?" I ask.

"Because it's nighttime," Ginny says sarcastically.

Priscilla laughs. Even Priscilla knows there's got to be a better explanation.

"It's called bioluminescent light," I say.

Priscilla likes it when I use big words, but Ginny acts like big words are no better than little ones. She doesn't need them. Ginny knows more about regular life than anyone I know, but when it comes to books, she won't even read a comic.

"So?" Ginny says.

"The males send out messages with their blinks," I say. "And the females of the same species send back the message and they mate."

"What if she's not the same speezes?" Ginny asks.

"*Species,*" I say. "Then the male stays away from her unless he's tricked."

"Tricked?"

"Fireflies never eat their own species," I explain, "but the females gobble up bugs from other families."

"Yuck," Ginny says. "Can you imagine somebody trying to eat Willie Bright?"

Both girls giggle like this is a great joke.

"That's not funny," I say. "He's a boy. Not a bug."

"He's a *welfare*," Ginny says. "That's another speezes. He wouldn't taste good."

I laugh, too, even though it doesn't feel right.

"But how *are* the boy fireflies tricked?" Priscilla asks. She likes the idea of tricking boys.

I explain how the females copy the blinking of other species. It's like a code, and they use it to lure the males in close enough to eat them.

Ginny bends over and peers into the bushes to see if any such activity is going on at the moment. "Who cares about lightning bugs," she says. "Where'd you learn this stuff, anyway?"

"From Lenny," I say.

"Ha. My dad says Lenny's a sissy," Ginny says.

I think for a moment about how I might better classify Lenny and it comes to me. "He's more like a scientist," I say.

"A scientist?" Priscilla says. "He dances like the girls."

"So?" I catch another bug and watch it crawl across my palm, flick out its wings, and take off. My hand smells like I've been holding nickels. I'll have to ask Lenny why fireflies smell like metal.

"So, he *is* a sissy," Ginny says. "Regardless." She swings on the railing to the steps and hangs underneath. It's too dark to see that smug look on her face, but I know it's there. I want to tell her that I'd rather be a smart sissy than a dumb jock like her brother Lewis. Lenny says Lewis Murphy can't even tie his shoes without looking at the instructions. We laugh about this, Lenny and me. We laugh about all the stupid stuff people do and say in Mercy Hill. Lenny says if he didn't laugh sometimes, he'd be bound to cry.

When the bandstand goes completely dark, we head for the picnic table where the women are sitting, waiting for the men to send their own messages, to say it's time to go.

"Someday we'll be sitting here watching *our* husbands play horseshoes," Ginny says proudly. "Won't it be great?"

I feel chill bumps slide up my arms in spite of the hot night. I can't visualize myself sitting under these trees talking about canning beans with some old versions of Ginny and Priscilla. Instead, I'm on a boat headed up the Rhine River, climbing the stairs of the Leaning Tower of Pisa, riding a train across France. I wish on the stars speckled across the sky above the floodlights. I wish the black night could alight like a moth and carry me away on its silent wings.

 ooking at the Stars...

"We live in the suburbs of Mercy Hill," Willie Bright says.

We take the shortcut through the woods, jump the stream that runs beside Miss Matlock's house, and slip through a space in the boxwood hedge.

"This is definitely not the suburbs," I say. The very idea makes me laugh.

"This is not town," he says. "And it's not a hollow."

"We live in a valley," I say, "a valley surrounded by hills. It's the country, for goodness' sakes."

"But—"

"A suburb has streetlights and sidewalks."

"Maybe not every suburb's the same," he says.

"The sky's lit at night," I tell him. "A suburb is close to a city and the sky stays lit up at night."

"How do you know that?"

"I've seen pictures."

"We have tons of stars to light up the sky here," he says.

I jump the porch steps and knock on Miss Matlock's screen door. "The suburbs have stars, too," I tell him.

"Stars?" Miss Matlock opens the screen door, wants to know what we're talking about.

I start to tell her that Willie thinks Persimmon Tree Road is a suburb but decide against it. She'd think I was making fun.

"We're all sitting under the same stars," Willie Bright says when Miss Matlock starts to pour the tea. "Don't matter where you live or if you're rich or poor. You've got the same sky."

"That's a good thought," says Miss Matlock. She smiles at Willie like he's a kindergartner who's just finished reading his first book. I want to say something smarter but can't think of anything.

"When you look at the stars, you're looking at the past," Miss Matlock says. "You're seeing space *and* time. Billions of years—gone but still visible."

"Like memories," I say.

Miss Matlock smiles, looks over her glasses. "Precisely," she says.

On the way home Willie Bright says to me: "If I was still a little kid and there really was a Santa Claus, I'd ask for a telescope."

"Wouldn't do you any good," I say.

"Why?"

"A telescope's way too expensive."

He looks down at his feet and walks faster, doesn't reply.

"It's way too expensive for me, too," I say.

rooping Flowers and Friendships...

I am a pretty little Dutch girl
My home is far away
I fell in love with a rub-a-dub-dub
Way down in the USA

The one to stay in the longest is the winner, so I stay in for all it's worth, even if I get blisters or get hit on the leg with a red-hot rope.

He asked me if I'd marry him
I said no no no no
He took me to his castle
And there I had to stay

The girls grab a second rope and I get doubles. You have to work both feet, each one at a different time, but it's like dancing. All you need is rhythm. Lenny says some people are born with it but some can't get it to save their lives.

Zeno Mayfield and his group of football players walk by just as I've made it to the end of the rhyme and he lets out a loud whistle. The other boys start laughing.

It's midsummer catch-up. Jump-rope team practice and football practice on the same field. Not a good idea. If their coach started practice on time, the boys couldn't bother us while we try to jump. It's hard to stay focused.

Jump rope's for babies, they say. But we're a team. We've won more blue ribbons than any school in our district. There are only three others—Jellico Springs, Willow Branch, and Ivy. Jellico Springs almost beat us last year, but Willow Branch and Ivy have never stood a chance. They're located way up in the hollows, where kids don't spend much time practicing jump rope. Still, we work hard at it and we're good.

After another round we take a break on the bleachers.

"Maybe I'll quit jump rope," Ginny says.

"Me too," says Priscilla. "I *really* want to be a cheerleader this year."

"You've already signed up," I say. "You can't quit the team now."

Ginny shrugs. "Miss Hart says we can."

I jump off the bleachers and head for the creek that runs alongside the ball field. Outside the place where the grass gets mowed, the field is full of wildflowers, yellow in spring, purple in summer, golden in the fall. In grade school we picked them for our teachers. Ginny, Priscilla, Chili. Murphy, Martin, Mahoney. The three Ms, three peas in a pod.

How can they do this? We'll never find anybody to take their places on the team. Not now. Not in the middle of the summer.

I hear footsteps and turn to see Zeno Mayfield stomping through the purple wildflowers.

"Hey there, Chili Pepper. Where you going?"

I say I'm taking a walk, picking flowers, if it's any of his business.

Zeno slides beside me and says if I let him kiss me just once, he'll give me his allowance for a month.

My face turns burning hot. I tell him money can't buy everything.

He stops and picks a purple flower, sticks it in front of my face. "So?" he says. "Is it a deal?"

"No. It's NOT a deal."

Zeno's eyes are big and wet, like a puppy's eyes. He

smells like Ivory soap. Still, I'd rather slap him than kiss him. I bend over and grab a whole bunch of flowers at once and head back to the bleachers with my hands shaking.

"What were you talking about with Zeno?" Ginny asks, twirling the ends of her blond hair around her finger. She looks like she's been set on a low sizzle.

"Nothing," I say.

"Did he ask if I like him?"

"He already knows the answer to that."

"Did he say he likes me?" Her look is hopeful and desperate at the same time.

"No," I say.

She puckers her lips like she's about to cry. "He didn't say he hates me, did he?"

"He didn't say anything."

"I saw him talking to you," she says. "I saw it with my own two eyes."

Her own two eyes are like darts, razor-sharp and aimed at me.

I shrug, stay quiet.

"What did he say?" Her words slip out with a hiss.

I turn to stone. Ginny can't see Zeno walking up behind her. She doesn't know he's there until he leans over her shoulder.

"I asked Chileda to make out with me," he says, his

words pouring into her ear like scalding water. He makes a kissing sound and runs back onto the field.

Ginny stares at me but doesn't speak. Priscilla and the rest of the team stare, too. I look down at the purple wildflowers drooping in my hands. Finally, Ginny stomps her foot.

"What does Chili have that I don't have?"

"Nothing," says Priscilla.

Nothing, nothing, nothing . . . the whole team agrees.

"He likes her," says Lily Lou Harris, her voice like a loud bell ringing in an empty church house. Lily's been on the team all year, but Ginny and Priscilla have never liked her much, never included her in anything outside of practice. She's in the fast group in class, the Triple As, always making perfect scores.

"What?" Ginny turns toward Lily and frowns.

Lily Lou shrugs. "I guess he just likes Chili better than you."

Ginny's face turns red and tough-looking, but her bottom lip starts to quiver. I look at her for a second and turn away like I don't notice. Lily inches closer to me, but the others stay put. The two of us are the oddballs in this group. We'll never be cheerleaders or May Day queens. Still, Zeno Mayfield wanted to kiss *me*. He would have given all his allowance for a month just to kiss me one time.

"I declined his invitation," I say, trying not to laugh.

"What?" Ginny looks confused.

"I said no."

Lily links her arm with mine and we leave the field together.

Volcanoes . . .

Miss Matlock names everything we're going to need in our packs.

"Water," she says. "This place we're going, the water's not fit to drink. We'll boil it first, then fill our canteens."

"What else will we need?" Willie Bright asks. He's down on his hands and knees using a trowel to dig up crabgrass.

"A warm sweater," she says. "It's hot in the valleys and cold in the mountains."

Every Friday Miss Matlock insists on coming up on the mountain to dig up clumps of weeds and clear briars from the pauper's lot. We don't have any of her books with us, so she's trying to describe the trip we'd be taking to the Andes Mountains if we were sitting in her parlor in a cool spot with the window fan running.

She says in that part of the world the mountains are so high, their heads are in the clouds and they're covered with snow and ice. Cotopaxi, she calls this place. A cone-shaped volcano belching up a rain of fire. And there are wide green valleys and high mountain lakes where the water sparkles like tinfoil.

When Willie finishes the crabgrass, we start pulling wild vines off the chain-link fence so the orange trumpet can grow. Miss Matlock says there are vines in the jungle that grow up the trees and strangle them. The tree rots away and the vine gets thick and hard and takes its place, but the tree's hollow inside. She once stood inside the shell of a vine tree, she tells us, and she could look up and see the sky.

"Wild orchids grow in the tops of the trees," Miss Matlock says. She takes the hoe and whacks at the stump that we've not been able to get out of the ground. Her face is turning red and her hair is wet with sweat. She's too old to be working in this heat.

I ask for some water so she'll stop whacking at that stump and take a break. Willie Bright follows us to the shade and pours himself a cup, too.

"What's there to see when you're climbing a volcano?" he asks.

"Birds," she says. "Coots and lapwings. And spectacled bears, too." She says these South American bears look like they're wearing glasses. Imagine: bears with glasses.

I glance at my watch. Momma's leaving work about now and the others will be getting home soon.

"I need to go," I say. "I'll get in trouble."

Miss Matlock pushes her hair away from her face, leaving a dirty smudge across her forehead. Her face sags, but her eyes are bright, almost dancing.

"We'll go to the Andes again," she says. "Or maybe the jungle next time."

Willie and I carry the tools to the truck and make sure we have everything we brought with us. The pauper's lot started out looking like a big, messy room, but Miss Matlock says it's now almost clear enough to imagine the possibilities.

We creep down the hillside, over the gravel and ruts, stirring up dust, until we get to where the pavement starts. I lean forward in the seat as if this will make the truck go faster, but Miss Matlock rides the brakes, lifting her foot only when it's about to stop. I feel stuck in place, like those faraway purple mountains with their heads in the clouds and their feet planted deep beneath the roots of the tallest trees.

Happiness...

"Happiness comes and goes like Wednesdays," says Mayme Murphy. She's Ginny's big sister, and today she's giving Myra a Toni home permanent so Myra doesn't have to go to the beauty parlor and spend a fortune to get her hair fixed. I'm sitting at the kitchen table watching Mayme twirl strands of Myra's blond hair around little pink curlers. When she gets close to the scalp, she puts a tiny sheet of paper around the curler and latches it tight. Every time she does this, Myra makes a face like she's been stuck with a pin.

"Happiness is getting this over with," Myra says, rolling her eyes at Mayme.

Mayme laughs and pats her on the shoulder. "It's gonna be worth it," she says. "Men won't be able to keep their eyes off you."

"I'm not looking for a man," Myra says. "It's too soon."

Jerry Wilson's just been gone a few months and Aunt Rose says Myra has to wait a year to look for a man. Besides, her belly's as big as a basketball.

"After the way he treated you all those years?" Mayme says. She holds a strand of hair in midair and bends over the back of the chair to look Myra in the eyes. "Why, you don't owe that man one month of waiting."

"Aunt Rose says it's not proper," I say.

"Phooey." Mayme shakes her head at me.

"But she says—"

"Don't make no difference what Rose says, little sister. She don't know what she's talking about." Mayme points a pink curler at me.

I don't like being stopped in the middle of a sentence. I look straight and hard at Mayme.

"Rose was right about one thing," I say. "She was one hundred percent right about that Mexican." I smile like saying "cheese" before jumping up from the table and hightailing it out the back door.

"She was not!" Mayme shouts. "You have no idea!"

I have more than an idea. I have the whole story, and so does everybody else in town. This is how it goes: Carlos the Mexican was heading to Delaware to work in the soybean fields when he got off the interstate in Mercy Hill and ran into Mayme Murphy at the Hamburger Hut. He was ordering four hamburgers, two large fries, and a chocolate milk shake when Mayme, big mouth that she is, made a remark to the thin air (because no one else was in line) that she didn't see where a little fellow like him put all that food. He turned around with a mean look on his face that melted instantly into a smile when his eyes met Mayme's and her beauty took his breath away. That's what Ginny told me back in the spring when she was still my best friend.

Ginny started using words that she'd learned from Carlos the Mexican. He was in love with Mayme, she said, so Mr. Murphy got him a job at the sawmill, and he stayed in Mercy Hill, living off the Murphy family, according to Pop, until it was time to pick strawberries in Florida.

Aunt Rose says you can't trust Mexicans. You've got to keep an eye on them. So, Mr. Murphy watched him like a hawk at the sawmill every day, but he left anyway. I saw him at the Piggly Wiggly the day he left town. Momma had sent me to buy dog food for Old Tate and Foxy Lady. It was like fate put me in that line.

"*Hola,*" I said, trying to talk Mexican like Ginny.

"*Hola, mi amiga,*" Carlos said. He was buying Pepsi "for the road," he said, holding up the six-pack and winking.

"Where you going?"

"I go f-a-a-ar away," he told me, stretching out the word like it was elastic. That's when I knew he was leaving Mercy Hill.

"Why?" I asked.

Carlos set the Pepsi on the counter and put his hands on my shoulders. I looked into his brown eyes and they did look kind of magical, the way Ginny said Mayme had described them.

"The longest river in the world wraps around my heart," he said.

He put one hand over his heart like he was about to say the Pledge of Allegiance and stood like this for a long time, staring at the mountain of Charmin toilet paper on display by the checkout counter. It was hard to tell where his mind was aimed.

Then he was gone, gone from the Piggly Wiggly parking lot and onto the interstate, taking his gold-toothed smile and his Mexican words with him because no one in Mercy Hill had any use for them.

Later Ginny told me about the argument. She'd heard him say that he didn't belong. "Why I stop here, anyway?" he'd asked Mayme. "I no belong."

I wish he'd stayed. I'd like to ask him if the mountains in Mexico are the same as they are here, if all the people look like him, if he ever saw the ocean.

Voices drift through the open window. Mayme sniffling and Myra telling her that I'm just a kid and don't know anything. Mayme says all she wants is happiness.

"That's all anybody wants," Myra says.

Myra thinks this hair permanent will change her life. The old Myra will be tossed out with the leftover blond hair that's lying on the kitchen floor, and the new Myra will come to life with a head full of springy curls. That's happiness.

I can see rain clouds slipping over the mountain. It's sunny on the porch stoop, but a wide band of white rain comes down on the distant hills, making them disappear. Momma says we need rain. It's been hot and dry for days and the garden is parched. The clay dirt in the backyard has cracks running through it like tiny earthquakes full of ants and roly-poly bugs. The bugs are taking cover now, slipping down through the cracks. They know the rain's coming even before Mayme and Myra know.

I turn up my face to catch the first drops. Today this is happiness. Cool rain on a hot face. I hold my eyes open for as long as I can before it starts to pour.

Quilts and VISTAs...

A VISTA worker is coming from Jellico Springs to look at Rose's quilts.

"Word got spread around about my sewing," Rose says. She tilts her chin just so. Momma sent me to help

Aunt Rose get her quilts down from the attic and display
them on the couch and the beds and the kitchen table.
Wedding Bands, Stars and Chains, Crows in the Pumpkin Patch, Around the World, Spinning Wheels, Flower
Gardens. And two Crazy Quilts made from pieced-
together scraps.

We sit on the front porch waiting for the VISTA
woman. Rose sews on a new square for her Dutch Girl
quilt and I read *The Cat in the Hat,* the only book my
aunt keeps out in the open. Her romance novels and
magazines are hidden in the bedroom closet, but I'm not
supposed to know about those. She always has me read
The Cat in the Hat aloud. She likes the rhyme and the
rhythm and the way the cat goes wild.

"This is a book for little kids," I say. "Don't you have
anything else we could read?"

"Nothing *we* could read," she says. "This is it."

"But don't you have—"

"I like the cat. Don't you like the cat?"

"Yes, but—"

"You'd better hurry up," Rose says. "Here comes that
quilt woman."

Rose is already laughing about the cat when the
VISTA woman walks up the porch steps.

I follow the two of them through the house. The
woman says all the quilts are pretty. *Unique,* she says.

Authentic. I remember these words so I can add them to my notebook.

It's hard to choose, she says, but she can only buy one today. She may be able to get Rose some other sales from her connections up North.

Aunt Rose tells her the name of each pattern, points out the quilting stitches in circles and squares and long, exact rows.

The VISTA woman goes back and forth a dozen times, unfolding and scattering the quilts here and there after we spent all morning fixing them. Finally, she pulls out an old, ratty quilt that's folded beneath the ones on display.

"How about this one?" she says.

Rose shakes her head.

"Oh, I like this one a lot," the woman says.

Aunt Rose looks away, wanders out to the front porch. The VISTA woman follows her and I follow the woman. Rose sits back down in her rocker and picks up the Dutch Girl pattern she's been working on.

"I'll give you two hundred dollars for this quilt," the woman says. She's unfolded it part of the way and is examining the fine stitching along the edges.

"That quilt's an antique," Rose says. "It's real old."

"Two hundred and fifty," the VISTA woman says.

"It's faded," says Rose.

"That's okay," says the woman. She's not about to give up.

"I made that quilt with my mother," Rose says. "Right before she got cataracts and couldn't sew anymore."

"How about three hundred, then?" the woman says. "I'll give you three hundred dollars cash for this quilt."

Rose looks up at the woman, her eyes moist behind her tortoiseshell glasses. I'm trying to think what's going on in her mind. Three hundred dollars will buy a lot. She could buy a suit like she's always wanted, a skirt and blouse and coat to match. Or get her hair fixed every month. Or trade her old washing machine in for one of the new harvest-gold washers she saw in the Sears catalog last week.

The woman digs in her purse for her billfold.

"That quilt is NOT for sale," Rose says.

And that's that. The VISTA woman stomps down the front steps and gets in her car and drives away.

"Money's not everything," says Rose. She pulls thread through the needle's eye and bites it off instead of using the scissors. "That quilt lasted a fire that took everything else we owned," she says. Rose knows where every square on the quilt came from—old church dresses, a threadbare tablecloth they used on the Christmas table, her dead brother's baby blanket, the one he couldn't sleep without. She keeps coming up with more reasons for keeping that old, ratty quilt even though I never once ask why.

When the Dutch Girl square is finished, Rose gets up and heads back inside.

"Let's go open a can of chicken noodle soup," she says. "You can finish reading me that cat book while it's getting hot."

 he Dancer...

Light shatters into colors as Lenny dances with his arms in the air. He's wearing Pop's green boxer shorts over his underwear and my yellow hairband on his head. It's stuck full of colored feathers.

Lenny's doing the "fancy dance" like the Cherokees performed at our school last winter. He got a book at the library that explained how it was supposed to be done and checked out the cassette tape that went along with it. It's mostly drum music with a flute that sounds more like a whistle.

Last week we bought two blue lightbulbs at the dime store, and tonight we put them in the lamps on each side of the bed and the room glows like a spaceship. Everybody's gone to the ball field to see Jack play in a summer scrimmage except Uncle Lu and he never comes down from the attic to check on us. It's a good thing. Ever since we broke Pop's light shade, dancing has been forbidden in this house.

Now the music plays and Lenny dances. Sometimes he puts me on his feet and we twirl around the floor together doing the fox-trot, the tango, or the rumba. Lenny checked out a dance book that shows diagrams of all the proper steps, and I let my legs go where his feet takes them. He says a dancer has to learn how to do all kinds of routines, not just dancing to rock and roll and not always with a partner. Tonight he's doing the "fancy dance" alone.

"Myra writes poems," I say when Lenny twirls alongside me.

"She does?"

"I've read them, but she doesn't know it."

"Are they any good?"

"I don't know," I say. "Maybe. They're mostly about a piano player."

"A piano player?" Lenny sounds like he wants to be surprised but isn't, like a person who knows the punch line before you've said it.

I take Myra's diary from the nightstand and open it to the page titled "Counter Melody." Lenny stops and reaches for the book like he's reaching for a hot skillet without a pot holder, but then he takes it and flips through the pages.

Overhead, Uncle Lucius stomps across the attic, causing my light to jiggle. Someday I expect him to jar it loose from its socket and send it falling down on top of me and Myra when we're sleeping.

I check the clock. It's almost time for the scrimmage to be over.

"We'd better put it back," I say, reaching for the book.

"Wait a minute," Lenny says. He sits reading while the light outside slips into the gloaming time. That's what Momma calls the edge of dark. The sky's already gone to deep blue when I see Pop's car drop over the hill from town.

"They're coming!"

Lenny tosses the book to me. "Take out those blue lightbulbs," he says. "I gotta go change clothes."

The second he grabs the doorknob, we hear Uncle Lucius stomping down the attic stairs.

"What's going on in there?"

"We're listening to music," Lenny says weakly.

"I don't hear no music."

The drums and flute have been finished for a while, but Lenny was reading and didn't pay attention.

When my uncle opens the door, Lenny is stuck in the blue glow of the lamplight.

"What in the world . . ." Lucius looks like he's swallowed a tooth.

Lenny stares at his feet so Uncle Lu can't see his lying eyes.

"Summer project," he says.

"A summer project?" Uncle Lu examines Lenny from head to toe, taking in his colored feathers and scrawny legs swimming beneath Pop's huge boxer shorts.

"My Cherokee *costume*," Lenny says finally, twirling around. "Do you like it, Lucius?" He stops, pulls back his shoulders like a soldier at attention, trying to look dignified in his outlandish garb.

Uncle Lu shakes his head at the two of us, and I feel like I'm going to faint, knowing he'll tell Pop and we'll be grounded for life.

But Lu turns around and starts back out the door.

"That costume's too big, Lenny," he says. "It's way too big for a boy like you."

Chili Supper . . .

Fireflies dance across the yard and a full moon floats above the treetops. Lenny says the moon is cold like ice and its seas are dry. A dried-up sea is like a desert, he says, but I've never seen the desert or the sea.

Outside my window Momma and Pop sit on the front porch talking, with the jar flies singing like a backup chorus. We just got home from the fried-chicken supper at the firehouse. Five dollars each, all you can eat, fried chicken till you turn blue in the face. I don't care if I never bite into another drumstick.

"They ought to ride her out of town on a rail!" Pop's voice rolls over the jar-fly chorus. He's talking about Penelope Winter, this girl from Pennsylvania who came here with VISTA. They're supposed to be helping the poor, but Pop says they spend too much time pitying people and teaching them how to get through life on handouts. Jobs are what we need in the hills, Pop says. Not pity.

"Her chili was not a bit better than anybody else's," Momma says. "Jimbo's puts it to shame."

"Trying to make a name for herself," says Pop. "That's all it was."

"By acting like we're all stupid? Like we've never even heard of chili?"

The uproar at the fried-chicken supper is still hot in their heads. Everybody was talking about some story this Penelope Winter had put in a Pennsylvania newspaper about how she'd brought her homemade chili to a potluck supper in Mercy Hill and the hill people were amazed. It was the first time we'd ever tasted chili, she said, making it sound like we were as dumb as rocks.

Jimbo's Cafe has been making chili for years, so old Jimbo and young Jimbo were fit to be tied when they heard this story. Then one of the Mason lodge men offered to make some contacts and get Jimbo's chili sold across the state. Maybe even take it into Tennessee and teach that Yankee girl a lesson. Hill people will tolerate being ignored and left out, but they won't stand for insult.

Pop says this is just like a VISTA. They like to show the dirt roads and the shacks and the barefoot kids on television and leave out everything that's good and pretty. We're not down here to promote tourism, they say, when anybody complains. But in these hills even kids with shoes go barefoot. We *like* to go barefoot. We get stung by honeybees till our feet swell up and turn red and itch like the dickens, but barefoot is who we are.

Momma agrees. "We didn't have much growing up, but we were always clean," she says. "Cleanliness is next to godliness."

She tells about Grandma making soap every fall when they killed the hogs. Big brown cakes of soap too slippery to hang on to, smelling like medicine. Pig fat and lye boiled in a round black pot in the side yard and Grandma with a red bandana tied round her head to soak up the sweat. "They never show poor kids sitting in a washtub," Momma says.

Pop laughs. "Northern folks think they're experts on poverty," he says. He spits out the word *experts* like it's made a bad taste in his mouth.

"We were as poor as Job's turkey," Momma says, "but I never *felt* poor a day in my life." She remembers the kids running up and down the stairs and singing together around the fire. Momma says a good life comes from a lot of different places. You can't buy a good life. You may as well keep your money in your pocket.

I listen at the window and turn it all over in my mind. When Myra comes in to write in her diary, I slip under the covers and daydream about traveling. Every week I choose a different place and think about that one place until I wear it out, until I've done in my dreams everything that I can imagine ever doing if I were to go there for real.

Tonight I go to Pennsylvania and I stand in front of the Liberty Bell, where everybody will be bound to take notice, and I make a speech. I tell them that the people of Mercy Hill, Kentucky, have been eating chili for a hundred years and it's way better than anything they'll ever put in *their* mouths.

 ## Sewing and Sweetness...

Aunt Rose sits on the front porch swing sewing on a baby quilt for Myra. It's hot and the carpenter bees are boring holes into the wood beneath the gutter, scattering dirty spots on the white paint like bird poop. When Pop comes home and sees this, he'll spray the holes with poison from the hardware store.

Rose doesn't notice the bees. She's humming "Rock of Ages" as she brings the needle up and down through the cotton pieces without even using a thimble. She never sticks herself like I do.

"You're good at that," I say.

"What?" Rose looks over her nose glasses.

"Sewing," I say. "You're good at it."

"The good Lord gave each one of us something to be good at," she says.

"What am I good at, Aunt Rose?" I look at her and wait, thinking how Jack can play ball, Lenny can dance, and Myra can write poetry.

Rose looks out toward Persimmon Tree Road like she's gazing at a plain white wall with no pictures on it.

"Well," she says, "you could be a real sweet girl if you didn't sass."

I look at the floor. *Sweet.* That's the last thing on earth I want to be. You can find sweet all over the place. Mercy Hill's cup is running over with sweetness.

"I don't want to be sweet," I say. "I want to go places."

Aunt Rose throws back her head and laughs out loud.

"Go places?" she says. "You want to be the mayor of Mercy Hill or maybe president of the USA?"

"No," I say. "I want to *really* go places, like travel to the other side of the world."

"No point in that," says Rose, looking back at her fabric.

"No point? What do you mean?"

"Daydreaming's a waste of time, Chileda. You ought to be a schoolteacher," she says. "They make good money."

"I want more than money," I tell her, but I'm not even sure what I mean by that.

"You have to have money," Rose says. "You've got to live."

"But I feel caught," I say. "I want to fly in a . . ."

"Caught?" Aunt Rose shakes her head and laughs again. "Darlin', we're all caught."

I admire her patience, the way she makes the smallest stitches and keeps them all straight. Every piece fits perfectly alongside the next. Still, each one is different. Green paisley, blue checks, bright red and purple solids. Rose turns them into wedding rings and flower gardens and maple leaves. Her special gift is sewing; it's having the fingers and the eyes and the heart to do something that would drive a person like me crazy.

You've got to live, she says. Those words pop around in my head like a whip cracking. She talks about making money and teaching school in Mercy Hill, but that last sentence, *You've got to live,* is the only one that makes any sense to me.

Collecting Pop Bottles...

I meet Willie Bright at the edge of the pine forest just as if we'd timed it, even though we didn't, and we head to Miss Matlock's house.

Halfway through the woods I see a blue baseball cap bouncing toward us. Zeno Mayfield. It's too late to turn around and go back. It's too late to tell Willie Bright to keep his mouth shut about where we're going.

Zeno breaks into the sunlight between tree shadows with a smug look on his face.

"Well, now," he says. "If it ain't Chili Pepper and Bright Eyes. Where're you two lovebirds headed?"

My face turns hot and I want to strangle Zeno. I can't let Willie answer him.

"The store," I say, realizing instantly that he'll know I'm lying.

"Are you sure? You're headed in the wrong direction," he says, wagging his finger in front of my face.

I look at that dirty finger and think: once I leave Mercy Hill, I will never have to see Zeno Mayfield's ugly face again.

"I'm collecting pop bottles to take to the store," Willie Bright says to Zeno.

"Pop bottles?" Zeno's suspicious.

"In the ditch over there," Willie says, pointing to the creek that runs alongside the pine forest separating the woods from Miss Matlock's yard.

"Why?" Zeno asks.

"To sell," says Willie Bright. "People throw bottles in the ditch and I sell them at Brock's store."

I push past Zeno and head down the hill.

"Don't run off," he says. "Think I'll come along."

I can't believe our luck.

At the creek Willie takes off his shoes and steadies himself on the rocks, placing one foot after the other like a tightrope walker.

"Come on," he says, waving to me and Zeno.

Some rocks stick up out of the water, sharp and slippery and covered with slime. At the end of the concrete culvert a heap of trash has collected and made a dam. Bottles are stuck amongst the tree branches and paper and plastic—mostly Pepsi and Coke and 7UP. There's a Fanta orange, too, and three Dr Peppers beneath an empty bottle of rubbing alcohol and a woman's pink hairbrush.

We collect the bottles—eighteen in all. Willie was clever to pull us out of this predicament, but he'll have to share his money with Zeno. What's worse is now Zeno knows about this ditch and he's sure to start taking all the bottles.

At Brock's store we split the money three ways and Zeno buys bubble gum. Willie puts his coins in his pocket and I do, too. When Zeno takes off toward the baseball field, he's all smiles, cracking bubbles like a cap gun.

I take out my money and offer it to Willie.

"Keep it," he says.

"But Zeno will start getting your bottles now and you won't have any money."

"It's okay," he says. "I know places you can find a ton of bottles. We go every Saturday morning."

"Who?"

"My family. We all go."

I think about Willie Bright wading barefoot through the creeks on Saturday morning picking up bottles from amongst Mercy Hill's weekly trash while I read and Jack runs and Lenny dances for real or in his head. I think of Saturday mornings with Myra and the baby-to-be sleeping with the shades down and Uncle Lucius stomping across our attic from one end to the other without going anyplace. I think about Willie Bright saying his is a different world, and he may be right.

Fishing and Fairies and Bugs That Kill Themselves...

First there's darkness without sound and then a bird calls and another and soon a whole chorus of birds starts singing. Light seeps in through the tree branches and melts the fog and moves like a ghost through the valley. Finally, you can see pieces of sky and the blue mountains in the distance. This is how morning comes to Mercy Hill.

I plow through weeds up to my knees, headed to the river with Uncle Lucius. I've got a book and he's got a fishing pole. The river's dark green, almost black, but it shimmers in patches where the sunlight falls. Uncle Lu says the light on the river is made by fairy dancers. Every time their feet touch the water it sparkles.

"I don't see any fairies," I say, looking down so Uncle Lu won't see me smile.

"Nobody can see them," he says. "You can only see the spots where their feet touch."

I don't care for fishing, but here on the riverbank it's quiet and cool and I can read in peace and not be disturbed by the television blaring or the screen door slamming or Aunt Rose coming over and giving me something boring to do while Momma's at work. Here Uncle Lu can pace the riverbank without making any stomping sounds. In the wettest places the mud squishes under his shoes, but the river flow drowns out even the squishing sounds.

Last night Myra was in one of her crying moods, talking about Jerry Wilson drowning and the baby coming and not knowing how she was going to make it, so Momma sat up with her till midnight. Myra can sit and watch game shows on television half the night, laughing and guessing the answers and complaining when the contestants miss easy questions, but the minute she turns off that set, she starts bawling.

I couldn't go to bed when she and Momma came into the room, so I went out on the front porch and sat with the bugs. A whole bunch of hard-shelled beetles went after the porch light over and over until they beat themselves to death on the screen door. This morning Momma swept a pile of dead bugs off the porch and into the azalea bushes. What makes a bug want to do something like that?

"What are you reading?" Uncle Lucius asks. He's standing with his fishing pole in one hand and a cigarette dangling from the other.

"Pride and Prejudice," I say. I start to mention that there were questions about this book on my state test last spring, that I later saw a copy on Miss Matlock's bookshelf and asked if I could borrow it. She just gave it to me, said I could have it for keeps. I almost let all this slip, but I stop talking in time.

"What's it about?" he asks.

"It's a love story." I hold up the book and turn the cover around so Uncle Lu can see it.

"Too much pride's a sin," he says. "You ought to be reading the Bible."

"I do. I read the Bible sometimes."

"If I was going to read, that's the *only* book I'd open,"

Uncle Lu says. He brings his line up out of the water, but there's nothing on it.

"Of course, you don't read much, do you?" I give Uncle Lucius a knowing look that could verge on sassy.

"Got better things to do with my time," he says, tossing the line back into the water.

I try to think of something Uncle Lu does that's better than reading a book, but I can't come up with anything.

"Like what?" I ask.

He thinks for a second while he's dragging on his cigarette.

"Fishing," he says. "Fishing's better than reading."

"Not in my book," I say.

He laughs and shakes his head. "You don't *have* a book."

 Home Alone...

They're all gone! This never, never, never happens.

Before we loaded up the house with relatives, I was alone at least once a week. I'd slip Old Tate and Foxy Lady inside and we'd chase up and down the stairs as free as whip-poor-wills until it was time for the others to come home. There was some excitement to this as Momma does not allow dogs in the house. They have fleas and drop hair and like to mark their territory.

This morning the dogs are stretched out asleep on the porch. I open the screen door halfway and call Old Tate, but he just cracks his eyes a wee bit and closes them again. Foxy Lady doesn't even bother to wake up. I guess I don't want to chase dogs through the house anymore anyway.

I pour a glass of iced tea and head upstairs. Being bored is not an excuse. Still . . .

Myra's diary is not on her desk. It's not lying open in plain sight where anybody could just glance over and read something by accident. It's not even in a top drawer with the pencils and paper and rubber bands that somebody else might need. It's all the way in the bottom dresser drawer beneath the stockings and underwear.

Myra's poems don't rhyme. Some are only two lines long. Others go on for pages. One verse is just a list of questions:

Will he come back someday?

Will he play, again, the songs I love to hear?

Will he ever see his gift to me?

Why doesn't she write it all out, tell the whole story? If I kept a diary, I wouldn't write nonsense verses that don't even rhyme.

Song of the Grasshopper . . .

We dig and hoe and rake and clip. Through thickets of brush and briars, wild-plum thorns and tangled roots. A yellow pumpkin sun overhead and headed west. Shadows lengthening down the hillside.

"It's sizzling hot out here," I say.

Willie Bright looks up at me with dirt on his face, a long-handled hoe in his hand.

"We're about done," Miss Matlock says.

The pauper's lot looks like it's been swept clean, bare as a board. It almost looked better when there was stuff growing here, when there were at least some wild green vines across the graves. But Miss Matlock insisted on stripping the whole lot before planting so the briars don't take over again.

She has Willie and me pull off the blue tarp from the truck bed and there's a garden of flowers in the back. Lavender and sweet alyssum and daisies. Blazing stars for the butterflies and Indian pink to attract hummingbirds. And there are lilies and sweet peas and red-hot pokers for the fence that separates this lot from the real cemetery. A yellow rose for the head of Willie's grandmother's grave. A white crepe myrtle that's just a tiny bush now but will someday be taller than us.

"We'll put the myrtle smack in the middle," Miss Matlock says.

Planting is a lot easier than cleaning. I don't have my watch today, so I keep an eye on the sun. I have to get home in time to clean up before Aunt Rose comes to cook supper.

Miss Matlock sits on the ground to plant.

"I can't bend over anymore," she says. "It's too hard on my back."

She sets the plants in rows and circles, gets up and steps back to look over it all, and has Willie and me dig up and replant the daisies. She wants the colors to mix just right. She wants this place to look like an English garden.

I'm tired and hungry and hot. I'd rather be in Miss Matlock's cool parlor looking at books and talking about traveling. These flowers will grow just as well whether the pinks are lined up beside the yellows or the reds or the whites.

I think she cares way too much about this lot. Maybe she's like Lady Macbeth, who Lenny's been reading about. He signed up for the advanced classes next fall and they have to read Shakespeare over the summer. He says Lady Macbeth is a kook, that she washes her hands a million times trying to get rid of her sin. Maybe that's what's wrong with Miss Matlock. She's trying to make up for running away from Mercy Hill. But what's that have to do with the paupers? With Willie's grandma Helena?

"Weeding will have to be done next spring," she says, looking at me. "You and Willie will need to handle it."

"What about you?"

"I'll help if I'm around," she says.

"Are you going somewhere?"

"No plans at the moment, but you never can tell."

"It'll have to be done *every* spring," Willie says. "Weeds always come back."

"I suppose it'll be a good project, then," she says. "It'll give the two of you something to do."

All around us the pauper's lot is blooming—red and yellow and green and purple. The lavender smells like perfume. The yellow rose has three perfect blooms, each petal curled around the stem just right with no flaws like the crepe-paper flowers we make for Decoration Day.

Miss Matlock looks up and smiles. "The ones lying here would be joyous if they could see how we've spent our time today."

Willie starts to say something, but she stops him, puts a dirty finger to her lips.

"Shhh," she says. "Listen."

We listen. To a rustling in the summer grass, a breeze full of imagined voices.

"What is it?" says Willie.

"Whispers," Miss Matlock says. "Whispers of the dead."

I look at Willie and he rolls his eyes. We quietly go back to planting, crumbling the hard clay earth over the last few lily bulbs.

Willie glances up every now and then and looks toward his grandma's grave, its metal marker covered with yellow petals and the green, thorny branches of the new rosebush.

"It's a grasshopper," I say.

"What?"

"That sound. It's just a grasshopper singing."

The Music Man Knocks...

A man stops by the house asking about Myra. He is tall and skinny, with red curly hair and little wire-rimmed glasses that keep sliding down his nose. I talk to him through the screen door and keep it locked. I wouldn't have answered except that Uncle Lu and Jack are both at home.

"Myra and the baby went to town," I say.

"Baby?" This fellow scrunches his eyebrows at me like I'm lying.

"Baby-to-be," I say, thinking I'd better make it clear.

"You m-mean? Well, Myra d-didn't . . ." He stutters and shuffles his feet and acts like I've told him the sky is falling. Myra's baby is old news. Everybody in town knows about it, so this makes me suspicious.

"Who *are* you?" I ask.

"A friend of Myra's," he says. He has a proper accent and is wearing bell-bottom blue jeans and a T-shirt with Bob Dylan's ugly face on it. His leather sandals have loops around the big toes. They're clearly hippie shoes.

"I don't know you," I say.

"Well, no," he says. "I've been gone awhile."

"Gone from where?" I ask. "You're *definitely* not from here."

He laughs and his eyes dance. They're blue like the flame on the gas stove. Hot blue eyes. I've never seen eyes like that.

"From Jellico Springs now," he says. "I teach at the college."

"Oh?"

He hesitates. "I'm originally from Wisconsin."

"Originally?" I say. I like the way that word bounces on my tongue. "Then Wisconsin's your true home."

He smiles and shows a set of perfect teeth. It looks

like he's about to say something else, but I decide to jump in first.

"If you're Myra's friend, how come you didn't know about the baby-to-be?"

He shrugs and stares. I stare right back. After he says *Well, let's see* twice, I decide to answer for him.

"You didn't know because you've been away for a really long time, right?"

"Right," he says. "I've been on sabbatical."

"What kind of word is that?"

"Sabbatical," he says again, and spells it like I'm in the first grade or something.

"Like the Sabbath," I say. "Like Sundays. You had a lot of Sundays."

"Yes and no," he says, and he starts laughing again. It's easy to make this fellow laugh.

"There's no such thing," I say.

"No such thing as *sabbatical*?" He raises his eyebrows.

"No such thing as an answer like *yes and no*. It's either yes *or* no. It can't be both."

"Sometimes it can," he says.

"Not in my book," I say. I wait for him to say that I don't have a book, but he just smiles and throws his head back to get his long hair out of his eyes. It's so curly it just falls right back into place.

"You should be in one of my classes," he says.

"What do you teach?"

"Philosophy. My students argue with me a lot. It takes a while to understand the yes-*and*-no answers to some questions."

I give him my best serious look. "Really?" I say. "Pop says it takes as long to become a fool as it does to become a bright person."

"And you're a bright person, I assume."

"Well," I say, "I'm sure not a fool." I decide to ask him the question that has been burning in my mind all summer, waiting for the right person to come along. This hippie teacher could be the mystery man. "Do you play the piano?"

He pitches me a puzzled look through the screen door.

"Sure, but why do you ask?"

"I knew Myra had a friend who played the piano but didn't know who he was. Now I guess I do."

"Now you do," he says, nodding.

That explains everything. And nothing. Myra's poems are about this man, this hippie teacher from Wisconsin who has played the piano for her in some other life she lives in secret. This new development will be rich news to Lenny's ears.

"What's your name?" I ask. It seems necessary now that I have this information.

"Drew," he says. "Drew Montgomery."

"I'll tell Myra you were here." I smile at Professor Montgomery and close the front door.

He turns around once from the yard, looks back, and squints in the sun. Then he drives away in a green Volkswagen. Nobody in Mercy Hill would buy a shrimp car like that. Pop says you may as well be riding in a baby buggy.

The Lives of Rocks . . .

"The music man came by to see Myra today," I say to Lenny.

We're sitting on the floor in the boys' room looking through Lenny's rock collection. He ordered something called a trilobite from a museum magazine that he picked up at the library. He says it's a prehistoric sea animal, but it looks like a bug to me, a bug that's been etched in stone. Pop says it's just a seven-dollar rock.

"The music man?" Lenny looks puzzled, but I know he's putting on. He's read Myra's poems, too, and I'm sure he hasn't forgotten them.

"That man Myra wrote about in her poem book," I say.

Lenny lines up the moonstones and geodes and the one red jasper.

"How do you know?" he asks.

"I saw him. He talked to me. His name's Drew Montgomery. *Professor* Montgomery." I tell Lenny how the professor stuttered and shuffled his feet.

"Why'd you open the door to a stranger?" Lenny says.

"Uncle Lu and Jack were here," I say.

"Did they see him?"

"Nope. Didn't even know he was here." I like it when Lenny can hardly believe what I'm telling him but knows it's true all the same. "He teaches philosophy," I say.

"I thought you said he was a music man." Lenny opens his rock book to a glossy page of agates and opals and topaz, acting like he's not much interested in what I'm telling him.

"A philosophy teacher can play a piano, too."

"You might be right," Lenny says. "Did you tell Myra?"

"No. Not yet."

Lenny points out a picture of some more pretty rocks. "Apache tears," he says. "I have some here." He takes some stones from a tiny blue velvet pouch.

"Why are they called that?" I ask, admiring the small round nuggets. They're greenish black and glassy and smooth to the touch.

"They're from lava," Lenny says. "Volcanic lava. When it pours into a lake or into the ocean, it cools and forms these rocks."

"But why are they called that?"

"Apache tears?" Lenny shrugs. "I guess because ancient people used them as tools or sometimes for their ceremonies," he says. "They get little bubbles of air and are smoothed by the wind and water. They look like real tears, don't they?"

I take a closer look at the little rocks. They could be beads or pieces of glass. Or tears, I suppose.

"What do you think Myra will do?" I ask, handing the nuggets back to Lenny.

"About what?"

"About that hippie college professor."

"He's a hippie?" Lenny's eyebrows jump.

"He wears sandals and ragged pants, and he's got long hair," I say.

"Your pop won't like that," Lenny says.

I'm looking over Lenny's shoulder, reading snatches of his rock book. It says on one page that over a billion years lumps of coal become diamonds, roses petrify, and blue stars die and fade away. Nothing ever stays the same.

"Wonder how Myra met that professor?" Lenny turns a clump of pages in the rock book and lands on a section about petrified worm poop. Yuck. "Who knows," he says. "But maybe it's a good thing."

"Why?"

"Jerry Wilson won't be coming back." He stops on a page full of diamonds.

"Diamonds come from plain old coal like we have in Mercy Hill," I tell Lenny. "It says so right here."

"And dinosaur bones sometimes turn to jasper," Lenny says with authority.

"Everything changes," I say.

"Yep. Everything changes."

Loose Threads...

I don't mention the professor until Myra's put on her nightgown and is sitting at the desk with her poetry book open. I look at her back and clear my throat like the school principal does before he makes an important announcement over the intercom.

"Guess who knocked on our door today?" I say.

"Can't imagine," says Myra.

"Drew Montgomery."

"Wha——" Myra turns around and looks at me with her mouth hanging open.

"He said he was your friend. A *good* friend."

"Well, I don't know . . . I mean . . ." Myra is holding a whole book full of her own words, yet she can't seem to find any to describe her friendship with the professor.

"Do we know any Montgomerys?" I ask. I look at her and wait for the answer like one of those men who host the TV game shows she likes so much.

"He's a professor at the college in Jellico Springs," Myra says finally, and she turns back around to her book.

"How come you know a professor?"

"I took a class last fall," she says. "A philosophy class."

"Do Pop and Momma know? Because——"

"No, they don't. And it's my business," she says. "Nobody else's."

"Momma likes it when you look like you're studying . . . when you're writing in your poem book."

Myra's eyes are suddenly filled with suspicion. It's like she's found a loose thread and she's searching back to see where the cloth started coming unraveled. She never told me this was a book of poems. She's always said she was writing about the baby. I can't let her know I read the book, have got to change the subject. . . .

"Professor Drew didn't know about the baby-to-be," I say.

Her face turns red in the lamplight. "You told him?"

I nod. "Was he Jerry Wilson's friend, too?" I think I know the answer, but I have to ask anyway.

Myra laughs. It sounds peculiar, like when somebody tells a joke and you don't get it but you have to laugh anyway to be polite. "No," she says. "Definitely not."

The room grows quiet. Myra stares at the opened poem book on her lap, and I stare at Myra, and the lightbulb in the lamp starts to flicker like it's going out. I'm hoping it does. I'm wishing the lamp would go out this very minute when the overhead's not turned on, when everything could go dark and all the questions floating around our heads could just fly out the open window.

Sphinx Moths...

A buzzing in the jasmine bushes catches Aunt Rose's attention and she leans forward and looks over the side of the porch.

"That hummingbird's back again," she says. "Look at it go!" The wings are a blur in the bushes.

Lenny gets off the porch swing and slips over to have a look. "That's not a hummingbird," he says. "It's a moth."

"A moth?" Aunt Rose puts down her quilt work, pushes her glasses up on her nose, and leans closer to the bush. "That's a hummingbird," she says. "I know a hummingbird when I see one."

Lenny shakes his head. "There're two of them," he says. "They're sphinx moths."

Aunt Rose clicks her tongue. "A smart boy like you ought to know the difference between a moth and a bird."

Lenny tries to explain why this little creature is a sphinx moth, but Aunt Rose refuses to listen.

"A moth looks like a butterfly," she says. "Not a bird. I know that much and I ain't even been to school."

Lenny hushes and sits and stares at the moth-birds.

After a while I slip over and sit on the porch floor beside him, and Aunt Rose goes back to her sewing. The jasmine bushes are covered with white tube flowers that look like snowflakes scattered across the green leaves. Every day at dusk these moth-birds come and buzz like crazy till dark, especially after a summer rain.

I lean over the porch and see the two little fliers amongst the flowers. Their bodies are reddish brown and fuzzy-looking. They're buzzing one minute and landing on a flower the next, sucking up the sweet nectar.

"What's a sphinx moth?" I ask Lenny.

"You're looking at two of them," he says.

I peek over my shoulder and see Aunt Rose shaking her head.

"How do you know?"

"Do you see how it sits on the flowers?" Lenny asks.

I nod.

"A hummingbird hovers," he says. "It doesn't stop and sit on the flowers." Lenny says a sphinx moth looks like a hummingbird and that a lot of people mistake them, but they're not birds at all.

"It's pretty big for a moth," I say.

"It's a big moth, all right," Lenny says. "And that fuzzy body catches pollen and spreads flowers."

"Will it spread these jasmine flowers?"

"Maybe," Lenny says.

The moon slips up over the top of the mountain on one side of the valley while the sun's disappearing on the other. Pretty soon Rose will have to take her sewing inside. We sit still and watch the moths buzz through the bushes, trying to eat as much as they can before dark. They don't simply fly from one flower to another. Instead, they buzz in the air for a long time before taking flight. Kind of like a helicopter.

"They're getting revved up," Lenny explains. "Sphinx moths can't just take off when they want to; they have to rev their engines and be patient until the time is right."

"How do they know when the time's right?"

Lenny looks at me and smiles. "They know," he says. "They always know."

"Where do they go?"

"Anywhere they want to go," he says. "Anywhere at all."

riendship, Past Tense . . .

I call, but Ginny's not home. Or she's busy, in a hurry, getting ready to go out. Where? Just out. Talk to you later, she says. Later never comes.

I call Priscilla.

"I'm sorry," she says. "Cheerleading takes time."

"What about our jump-rope team?"

"That's *yesterday.*"

Yesterday and today and tomorrow. Miss Matlock says when you get old, it all runs together like one long, crooked river.

Priscilla, Ginny, and Melody Reece hang out at the

bandstand in town. Two Ms and one R. Two peas and a bean in a pod. A new configuration, Miss Matlock says. These things happen.

I put *configuration* in my red notebook. *Pattern, arrangement, relationship.* I list only synonyms now. You can't learn nearly as many words if you have to learn long definitions. Synonyms are like windows to peek through so you don't have to memorize what the whole room looks like.

Sometimes the other cheerleaders are at the bandstand, too. Sometimes Zeno's there with the football boys. The girls giggle in their own huddle, pretending to have secrets and dying for the boys to ask so they can tell. The boys lean over the sides and sit with their feet dangling above the azalea bushes.

I look the other way when Momma lets me out of the car to run to the Custard Corner and get Uncle Lucius a brown derby ice cream. On the way home we roll up the windows so the wind doesn't melt it, and Momma breaks the speed limit twice, three times. I hold on to my seat around the curves.

One day at the Piggly Wiggly, Melody Reece was wearing Ginny's sandals. Last year *we* traded. I wore those sandals for a whole week. They're light-brown leather, a color that fades away into the skin. Thin straps. Expensive. Ginny's mother ordered them from a catalog and they cost more than regular shoes. That's why Momma said I could *not* have a pair. You don't pay all that money for a few straps.

I stopped in the aisle that day holding a head of iceberg lettuce and a dozen eggs with my eyes hooked on Melody's feet. Her toenails were painted neon purple and this completely ruined the natural effect of those sandals. Suddenly I realized—this is how it happens. One day you occupy a spot in a pea pod where you trade shoes and T-shirts and secrets, and the next day your spot goes to somebody else.

 ictures and Symbols . . .

"Let's go to the movies," I say to Lenny.

It's Saturday morning and Myra's getting ready to go to Jellico Springs to clean the room that will be a nursery if she ever moves back there. For breakfast Aunt Rose brought over a dozen of her homemade cinnamon rolls straight out of the oven and we ate them all. Now she's washing the dishes while Momma dries.

"Nothing good's playing in town," Lenny says.

"Myra can drop us at the Rex in Jellico Springs," I say. "They've got a new movie on called *Blowup.*"

"That's not a new movie," says Lenny. He listens to the movie reviews on his transistor radio late at night when our stations go off and the distant ones hit the airwaves. He says all the movies are old by the time we get them.

"So?"

Lenny nudges me out of the kitchen and down the hall to the living room. "Besides," he says, "that movie's not for kids."

"I'm not a kid."

"You're too much of a kid for that movie," he says.

"Have you seen it?" I know he hasn't. I know everywhere Lenny's been.

"No," he says. "But I heard some man talking about it on WOWO a few years ago. Even then it was old. *And* for adults."

"I'll go by myself," I say, and I turn and head back to the kitchen, knowing full well that Momma will not let me go to the movies alone.

Lenny hears everything on WOWO or WCAO or WLS, stations in the big cities, a million miles from Mercy Hill. He imitates the disc jockeys, tries to speak with a Yankee accent, walks around the house talking in slogans: *It takes two hands to handle a Whopper.* We don't even have fast food in Mercy Hill. Only on television.

Myra drops us in front of the Rex. She thinks we're going to Theater 2 to see *Planet of the Apes,* which is not
brand-new either but newer than *Blowup.*

Lenny says I should try to look older.

"How do I do that?"

"Stand up straight," he says. "Maybe tiptoe."

We get the tickets easily because the ticket woman
has her baby in the cage with her and it starts bawling
about two seconds before Lenny steps up and asks for
two tickets. She doesn't even give me a glance.

We go in and sit in the dark beneath a huge rectangle
of faint blue light. Lenny goes back out for Sugar Babies
and Cokes and my eyes start to adjust. I see a few heads
in front of us and to the sides. No kids, that's for sure.
Lenny said the college ordered this movie for their summer English classes to see. Otherwise, it would not be
shown in this neck of the woods. That's how Lenny put
it. This only adds to the excitement. I straighten up so
my head will be as high above the seat as all the others'.

First we get a *Roadrunner* cartoon and now previews for
The Sound of Music, which was showing last summer and
the summer before that. Myra brought me twice to see it.

"That's the symbol for my life," Lenny says, staring at
the images sweeping across the big screen.

"What?" I ask. "What's the symbol for your life?"

"Dancing," he says. "My life, my momma's life. Dancing is everything."

Some people in front of us turn around in their seats and stare.

"If you just want to dance," I whisper, "why did you sign up for the advanced classes next year?" Lenny's having to read Shakespeare all summer and I can't imagine that's something he needs to know to be a dancer.

"Getting smart gives you a route," Lenny says.

"A route?"

"A road to someplace," Lenny says. "That's what the counselor told me. She said I needed a challenge and a direction."

I think about Miss Stone, our guidance counselor, sitting behind her desk with a fat folder full of test scores and making those little grunting sounds of disapproval that she has a habit of making.

"She tells everybody that," I say.

"Well, maybe some people listen."

Shhhh! Heads whip around and give us mean looks as the blue lights above us start to dim.

The film is slow. A photographer takes pictures. A lot of pictures. Spends a long time developing them, looking at each photo from different angles, blowing them up.

And there are drugs and all sorts of bad behavior going on. And maybe a murder. But maybe not.

"See?" Lenny says when it's over. "I told you."

We walk outside into bright sunlight. I blink and look around for Myra.

"What?" I ask.

"I told you this was not a kid movie."

"It was quite interesting," I say, hoping he doesn't ask me to explain anything about it.

"'Quite interesting'?" Lenny laughs. "You don't have a clue," he says. "I didn't understand half of it myself."

"Was there really a murder?" I ask. "Could you really see that in the picture the man took?"

"Who knows," says Lenny. "We should have seen the apes."

"I saw it last year."

"Yeah . . . me too."

We sit on a park bench across from the theater and wait for Myra. She is thirty minutes late. Lenny takes out his wallet and opens the secret compartment behind the place for dollar bills and pulls out a photograph.

"Who's that?"

"My mother," he says. "That's my mom."

The picture is black-and-white, wrinkled down the center like it was folded at one time, and faded. The woman is wearing black short pants with a white blouse and a little black jacket. Net stockings, high-heeled shoes, and a tall hat. She's dancing on a stage somewhere, Lenny says, but you can't really see the stage or the lights or the audience. You just know they're there.

Paradise...

I've come with Aunt Rose to the top of Mercy Hill Mountain and we're sitting in the spot where the dining room of Grandma Sudie's old house used to be. "The old home place" is what Rose calls it.

We've come up the mountain looking for goldenseal plants so Aunt Rose can make a salve to put on Uncle Lu's arm where he scraped it on a barbed-wire fence, which caused it to turn all red and puffy.

"This'll take out the infumation," Rose says, holding up her bag of wild plants.

"Inflammation," I correct her.

"Same thing."

Rose is stubborn. She is not educated, but she has an answer for everything. Life learning is better than book learning, she claims.

This morning she packed pimiento-cheese sandwiches and Dr Peppers in a brown bag, so we're having lunch in the sun.

"It used to be paradise here after a rainfall," Rose says, holding out both arms like she's reaching for the past.

"Paradise?"

"The roses," she says, pointing to an old garden gone wild, one red rose plant climbing like a vine all the way to the top of a dogwood tree. "After a good rain they'd glisten in the sun," she says. "Red, yellow, pink, white. Momma planted every color that spring."

I take a bite of my sandwich and when I look back at Rose, she's staring off into space, moving her mouth without making a sound.

"Are you praying, Aunt Rose?" She does this at the supper table when we start eating before the blessing.

"Nope," she says. "I'm talking to Momma."

"You're talking to Grandma?" I want to laugh because I think maybe she's joking, but then I see she's not. She smiles, closes her eyes, and takes deep breaths like you have to take at the doctor's office so he can listen to your lungs.

"Momma didn't like the hard rain because it beat down her flowers," Rose says, opening her eyes now and looking at me. "But I liked the way raindrops looked on the petals. Like tiny jewels."

She holds out her bare hands, the nails dirty from collecting goldenseal, and tells me she used to dream of owning a real diamond ring.

It gets as still and quiet as a rock.

All of a sudden a big bird comes whooshing through the poplar trees. A hawk, maybe. Looking for baby rabbits or striped chipmunks. Aunt Rose doesn't even notice; she's still looking down at her hands. I need to bring her back to the old garden, make her smile.

"I'll bet the roses were pretty back then," I say.

"I remember the day Momma planted them," Rose says. "But I wish I could remember how she looked."

"How she looked?"

"I can see her working out there as plain as if it was yesterday, but I can't see the look on her face."

The rose garden has been taken over with briars, all the colors swallowed up by the dying summer grasses. Sun-dried silk from the milkweed floats in the air with the dragonflies, drifting above the lost flowers like messages on the wind.

"Tell her I'm here, too," I say.

"What?" Aunt Rose looks at me like I've opened the door to her hiding place.

"Tell Grandma there's no rain today. Tell her the sunlight's everywhere."

 **M**ean Streaks...

Mayme Murphy bangs on the front door. I run down the stairs as quick as I can so she doesn't wake up Myra and Uncle Lu. Momma and Pop have gone to work, Jack's out running, and Lenny's in the backyard studying ants. It's almost ten o'clock.

"Where's Myra?" Mayme says when I open the door. She looks around me and up the stairs.

"In bed," I say.

"Get her up," Mayme says.

"Why?"

"Just get her up!" Mayme pushes her way into the house and stands in the living room wringing her hands. "Well?" She looks hard at me. "Go on!"

I don't like it one bit when somebody outside the family tries to tell me what to do, especially Mayme. She always bosses Ginny around. But there's something big in the air this morning. I can feel it. I stomp up the stairs, mostly to irritate Mayme but also to let Myra know I'm coming.

Myra drags her big belly out of bed and slips on her floppy pink house shoes and the robe that won't button anymore.

"I've got to wash my face," she says, and heads for the bathroom.

"No you don't!" Mayme calls up from the foot of the stairs. "You need to come down here right now."

Myra holds the railing and clumps down the stairs and I stay right on her heels. I wouldn't miss this for the world.

"What's wrong?" Myra asks when we get to the bottom.

"Let's go in the kitchen," Mayme says, acting like she's in charge of the morning.

Myra sits at the table and Mayme goes over and pours the leftover coffee in two mugs just like she's at home.

"Chileda, you need to go out back and play," she says.

"Play? I don't play."

Mayme looks at Myra and Myra lowers her eyebrows at me, so I get up and go out back, but I leave the door open so I can hear.

Lenny comes around the house with his ant book and magnifying glass and I tell him to be quiet and sit down. We listen to Mayme pace back and forth. Stomp, stomp, stomp. Like she's holding the news inside until the last second.

"Jerry Wilson is alive!" she says at last. "He's living in Myrtle Beach."

We hear Myra gasp.

Mayme says that Eva Lou Perkins, Myra's doctor's nurse, saw him with her own eyes. She went over to Myrtle Beach with two girlfriends last week and rented a room in the Holiday Inn. They got good tans, Mayme says, and ate funnel cakes every day and rode the biggest Ferris wheel you can imagine. She keeps on and on about Eva Lou's vacation until Myra screams at her to stop.

"It can't be him," Myra says.

"They talked to him," says Mayme. "And he was with a woman, a black-haired woman." Mayme says they were hugging up together right on the boardwalk in front of everybody and that this was one of the prettiest women Eva Lou had ever seen.

Myra starts crying.

"You're pretty, too, sweetheart," Mayme says. She tries to sound like she didn't mean to tell Myra about this woman's beauty, but, of course, that was the main thing on her mind when she stepped in the door. Ginny's like that, too. Mean streaks run in that family. That's what Aunt Rose says. She knows all the women relatives back to Ginny's grandma.

Mayme tells Myra that everybody in town knows about Jerry.

Lenny laughs out loud. "Of course they do—with somebody like her to blab it," he says.

All of a sudden we hear Mayme come stomping

down the hallway. She slams the big door to the porch so we can't hear.

We sit for a long time listening to the birds and cicadas singing.

Trees...

I ask Lenny to name as many trees as he can, and he thinks on it for a minute and comes up with twenty-two, including fruit trees. He doesn't name any of the trees I've seen in Miss Matlock's books about the Amazon rain forest. They're my favorites.

"Do you know what a cecropia tree is?" I ask.

Lenny shakes his head.

"Acacia?"

Lenny says no.

I mention alder and fig and mangrove, but Lenny isn't sure about any of these trees. I tingle at the thought that I finally know more about something than Lenny does.

"Maybe fig," he says. "Fig I've seen."

At suppertime Lenny brings a tree book to the table. He's checked it out of the library.

"I found your trees," he says. "They're mostly in the jungle."

Momma looks at me. "What are you talking about?"

"Just trees," I say. "Me and Lenny are interested in trees."

Pop looks over his glasses. "For what purpose?"

"Just to know," I say.

"For goodness' sakes, it's summer," Pop says. "Put those books away and go climb a *real* tree. You're not even in school." Pop gets frustrated about Lenny having his nose in science books all the time instead of doing sports or mowing the yard or trimming the bushes. Pop says Lenny's too pale and he's going to keep me inside and make me sickly-looking, too.

At the other end of the table Uncle Lu's holding a fried chicken leg out in front of him like he doesn't know what to do with it.

"Trees," he murmurs, staring at the chicken. He shakes his head and puts the leg back on his plate without taking a bite.

"Why are you interested in jungle trees?" Momma asks. She throws me a suspicious look, but I shrug and go back to eating.

"I read about a tree in Kentucky that owns itself," Lenny says.

Jack laughs. "Does it own a car, too?"

Lenny ignores him. He says two women decided they wanted to save it, to make sure it couldn't ever be cut down, so they made up the legal papers to let it own itself.

"How crazy can a person be?" Pop shakes his head. On the word *crazy* we all look over at Uncle Lu without thinking.

"It's a sycamore," Lenny says, "a sycamore tree over in Knott County. It's had its papers since 1918."

"I was born before that time," Lucius says proudly. "I've got papers to prove it." He's eating one green pea at a time, like they're pills. He picks up a pea with two fingers and pops it into his mouth. Then he takes a drink of water and swallows the pea whole.

"Eat your chicken, Lucius!" Momma taps her fork on her plate to get his attention.

It's seems strange without Myra at the table. The last two days she's gone over to Jellico Springs to have dinner with "friends." But she doesn't say what friends or why. No one mentions Jerry Wilson's name. That would be like cursing.

Outside our dining-room window the maple tree is full of green summer leaves. It could almost be a fig tree in the jungle, full of parrots or monkeys or bats. And I could be riding a boat on the Amazon River. Someday, maybe.

 ish and Flowers...

"You can never have too many flowers," Miss Matlock says. She's sitting in her rocking chair on the front porch, her eyes set on the vine of moonflowers climbing up the tulip poplar tree. Her hands are small and delicate lying in her lap, and her hair flies loose from its bun.

I'm on the top step and Willie Bright is leaned up against one of the white columns, whittling a sycamore stick into a sharp point like a pencil.

"What are we gonna do today?" he asks. It's a hot-summer, middle-of-the-day, nobody-home kind of bore-dom. When the sun goes down, we'll both have to work in the garden. I'll be in the tomato patch dusting for bugs while Willie's in the bean field. Pop gives Willie all the beans the Brights can eat plus two dollars an hour to help Jack and Lenny.

"How about going underwater?" Miss Matlock says.

"Underwater?" Willie scrunches up his face.

I wait to hear more.

Miss Matlock gets up and goes inside, so we follow her. In the parlor she digs through a stack of *National Geographic* magazines until she finds the one she's looking for.

"Let's have some warm gingerbread with cream," she says, and she goes off to the kitchen to put on the teakettle. Willie Bright can't wait to eat. Sometimes I think he comes to Miss Matlock's house just for the snacks. Momma says those Bright kids are bony and look dark around their eyes. I study Willie's face when he's not looking, but his eyes seem fine to me. Nice, even.

In the other room the mixer roars to life, whipping up cream with vanilla and sugar.

"Where're your friends?" Willie asks. "Ginny and Priscilla?"

"They're at cheerleading camp," I say. I decide not to mention that I don't really see Ginny and Priscilla much anymore. Only at church.

"You didn't want to be a cheerleader?"

"Nope. Not me."

Ginny and Priscilla got on the yellow bus with the other girls on a hot Saturday morning. I was standing on the courthouse square, but I didn't wave. I wasn't jealous—at least, not jealous of them for being cheerleaders. I didn't wave because I didn't want them to go. I didn't want them to get onto that yellow bus with their suitcases and leave town before me. It's not fair.

That morning Momma had sent me into town with
Uncle Lucius so I'd make sure he knew how to get back
home. He wanted an ice cream cone at eight o'clock in
the morning, so he banged on the window at the Custard Corner for ten minutes before the custard lady got
tired of hearing it and opened up an hour early just to
dip two cones. We both had brown derbies, soft vanilla
dipped in chocolate that hardens. Then we watched the
bus leave with the cheerleaders.

Willie Bright smiles when Miss Matlock brings
in the warm gingerbread. She sits between us and
opens the magazine to a mass of silver fish swimming
in the same direction, forming a wall under the bluest
water I've ever seen. The straight-up sun in the picture is like a camera flash piercing the surface above
the fish.

She turns the page and names the fish we're looking
at—orange and white clown fish; sharks and flat
stingrays; and purple parrot fish with spots. Schools of
fish that you would never find in the Cumberland River.
And the pretty flowers under the water are not flowers
at all, Miss Matlock explains. They're living coral, a million tiny animals stuck together, never going anyplace.

"Like the people in Mercy Hill," I say.

Miss Matlock shakes her head and turns away, but I
see her smiling.

Willie and I take the long way home, across the meadow and over the rattling old footbridge to the bottom of the riverbank. We stand and let the water run over our toes. It's dark green, almost black. Not clear like the blue water with the pretty fish. Miss Matlock says the blue-water oceans have white sandy beaches where it feels like you're walking in talcum powder, but this riverbank is muddy and the bed of the river is full of rocks.

Willie wades out first and I follow him. When we get to the spot where the water is waist deep, it's hard to stand. The river rushes by like it's in a hurry to get on to the next place.

We steady ourselves and sit down at the same time, holding our breaths and letting the cool water rush over our heads. It roars and gurgles and cuts out bird sounds and the dogs barking in the woods. I open my eyes and look around, but it's all brown and dark and spooky like being in a cave. There are no pretty fish or flowers or bright sunlight shooting daggers through the water.

We pop up to breathe. Somewhere a blue jay squawks in the willow trees.

"You want to do it again?" Willie asks.

"Nope. I think I'll just dry out and go home."

At the edge of the river there's a big flat rock that

heats up in the sun. It's where I sit and read sometimes when Uncle Lu is fishing. I climb up on the rock and stretch out, squint my eyes against the bright light. Little round drops of water on my eyelashes make rainbows. Rainbows on the river, in the trees, across the sky. I can hear Willie Bright dunking under the water and coming up again and again, looking for flowers and fish and colors that are never going to be there.

I think about this river running into other rivers and all the way to the sea. I turn over and spit into the water and watch that blob of spit head for the blue ocean.

 Polaroid Days...

Lenny has a camera called a Polaroid. It used to be Uncle Roscoe's and it still works. You snap a button and it spits out a picture. They're black-and-white and fuzzy-looking, but Lenny says they'll get better when he becomes more expert at it. He takes pictures of ripe watermelons and bushels of green beans.

"What about the cornfield?" I ask. "Don't you want a picture of the cornfield?"

"You take it," he says, handing me the camera. He shows me the little window to look through and which button to push.

Even at a distance the cornfield takes up nearly the whole frame. Green stalks with yellow tassels wave in the breeze under a wide stretch of turquoise sky. I see gold, green, blue, and all the other colors that won't show up in the picture, the stalks leaning away from the wind.

Miss Matlock says in all of nature this is so. A tree bends but snaps back when the wind stops blowing. The river stays its course until nature sends a raging flood, and the sands of the desert swirl and settle wherever the wind wills. Sand doesn't refuse to fly, and the river can't leap its banks under its own volition.

When Miss Matlock used the word *volition*, I went straight home and looked it up in the dictionary. Each time I go to her house, I come home with a new word. *Volition* sounded like one I wanted to remember. It's a word that can head out on its own.

I snap the picture of the cornfield as a rain cloud edges toward the sun. When the photograph slips out, the stalks are brightly lit with sunshine. You can't tell that it's about to rain. Photos can only tell you so much. You can't see the seconds before or after the snapshot.

Lenny pastes my photograph with his in a yellow notebook.

"What's that?" I ask.

"A memory book," he says. When he's gone from this place, he'll still be able to see the watermelon on the vine and the cornfield before the rain.

"Why would you want to do that?"

I always figured Lenny would leave and not look back, but he says even when your number-one goal in life is to leave a place, you might still want to remember it.

*B*acon, Beans, and Gumdrops . . .
We've been picking beans all day—Jack, Lenny, and me. And Willie Bright, too. We've got Kentucky Wonders growing wild like jungle vines.

When we come out of the field, Momma says she needs bacon to put in the beans. Bacon and onions and vinegar. I can already taste them—long, green, and curvy, with brown seeds inside. We'll have corn on the cob and fresh tomatoes and watermelon, too. Everything off the vine or plant or stalk. It's a no-meat night, except for the bacon.

"Can you run to the store for me, Chili?" Momma says.

"Run?" I'm so tired I don't think I could run ten feet.

"You know what I mean."

Jack and Lenny still have corn to gather and everybody else is too busy to "run" anywhere. Myra's propped on her pillows in front of the television in a yellow top that's too tight. Her belly looks like a balloon about to explode. Uncle Lu's fishing and Aunt Rose is helping Momma cook. So I'm it.

Willie Bright goes with me to Brock's store so he can get one of his dollars changed and buy something for his little brother and sister. Maybe candy.

I ask Mrs. Brock to slice the bacon extra thick. Momma likes to cut it in sections so the beans can soak up the juices from the chunks.

I'm standing at the meat slicer when I see Ginny and her sister, Mayme, come in the store. I know Ginny spots me the minute she rounds the counter, but she turns and keeps talking to Mayme like she doesn't even know I'm there.

When Willie comes back with his bag of candy, we get in line to pay behind old Mr. Epperson, who's talking loud, complaining about the price of corn. He can't plant a garden anymore, he says, and he can't keep paying these skyrocket prices. He's on a fixed income, whatever that means. I want to tell him to go by our house and get some corn because we've got plenty, but

Mrs. Brock might get mad because that would lose them a sale, so I just keep quiet and wait.

"How's your sister?" Ginny asks. She and Mayme have moved in line behind us with a box of white-sugar doughnuts and milk. They're both wearing lipstick like they're going someplace special, and Ginny's had her hair cut and curled in the same style as Mayme's. They look like twins ten years apart.

"She's fine," I say. I turn back around and see Will Epperson paying with quarters and dimes, taking his time.

"When's that baby coming?" Ginny asks. She's chewing bubble gum and doing the hair-twirling bit she always does with her finger. "Do you know yet?"

"Pretty soon," I say. "September."

"*Aunt Chili* . . . that sounds too weird," says Ginny. She's got lipstick on her teeth.

I don't know what to say. I haven't thought much about becoming an aunt. So far I've just thought of the baby as Myra's, but it's going to be one more added to the family. "I guess it's okay," I say. "Being an aunt is okay."

"Well, I can't wait for school to start," says Ginny. "I'm *totally* bored."

I nod even though I'm not anxious to go back to school. I like the summer. Ginny looks past me. "How

about you, Willie Bright Eyes? I heard you were getting held back." She grins, looks from Willie to me
and back to Willie. "Think you'll ever make it to the
eighth grade?"

I want to say something to support Willie, but the
words won't come. Maybe it's because Mayme's standing
right behind Ginny, waiting to say something that's even
meaner. Or maybe I'm just a plain old coward.

Willie turns to face them with his shoulders
straight and his hands in his pockets. "That's the plan,"
he says.

I inch ahead until my nose is right at the hunched-
over part of old Mr. Epperson's back. I can't wait to get
out of this line and go home.

When we finally start out the door, I turn around
and see Ginny searching for something in her straw
purse. It looks brand-new.

Willie's walking with his head down.

"I'm sorry I didn't . . ."

"Who cares," he says.

Down Persimmon Tree Road we go with our bacon
and candy. Willie Bright opens the bag and offers me
some gumdrops. I choose three. Red, purple, and green.
Strawberry, grape, and lime—my favorite flavors. Willie
takes three for himself, all yellow lemon because the little kids don't like lemon.

inseng...

Late August sunrise turns the sky from red to gold.

Uncle Lucius is dressed all in green, standing in the backyard with a bag and a hoe. He's headed to the woods to hunt for ginseng. It can cure anything, Uncle Lu says. It's the best medicine in the world.

I've seen him stop in the woods like he's in a trance, bend down beneath the spicebush and goldenseal, and clear away the brush from the clusters of ginseng leaves with their tiny red berries. He drags his hoe gently around the fibers, like he's operating on a baby, to get at the round, knobby roots that can cure anything. It's as if my uncle can smell the seng or somehow feel its presence.

Patches of ginseng hide all over these mountains and most people walk right by and never notice a sprout. The Cherokee believe ginseng makes itself invisible to those unworthy of it, Uncle Lu says. But he always spots it. My great-grandma on Pop's side was a Cherokee, so worthiness runs in the blood.

People in China will pay good money for ginseng. They're desperate for it, according to Uncle Lu. They lay it out like gold on green-velvet cloths in the marketplace. I wonder what it would be like to travel the route of the seng, to go all the way to China on a copper-bottomed boat and know people at the other end were desperate to see you.

Selling Candy...

The boys come to our house after football practice—Joe Ed, Calvin, and Darby. Jack's new friends. They're seniors and Jack's just a sophomore, but the coach says he's all-star material.

They sit at the kitchen table drinking Pepsi out of the bottle. Calvin pours a pack of peanuts in his bottle and crunches a mouthful every time he takes a drink.

"That family was rich," Darby says. "They left her that big house."

"Who?" I ask. I'm washing dried pinto beans in the sink so Momma can soak them overnight.

"That old crazy woman who lives down the road," Jack says.

"Old Miss Matlock," says Calvin.

"They weren't rich," Joe Ed says.

"Rich for Mercy Hill," says Darby.

"I still don't think we ought to go to that house," says Joe Ed. "I don't care if she *is* rich."

"Why would you go to her house?" I turn around and face the boys.

"We're selling candy bars for the football team," Jack says. "We need to sell forty boxes by the time the season starts."

"My pop says she's lived around the world," Calvin says.

"That old woman?" Joe Ed snickers. "I'll bet she's never been out of Kentucky." They all laugh.

"Honest," Calvin says. "It's the truth. She ran off when she was young. That's what Pop told me."

"How does he know?" I ask.

"Go play, Chileda." Jack tries to sound bossy.

"Momma told me to fix the beans," I say, throwing him a look that could melt a rock.

"Pop knows," Calvin says. "He remembers."

"Didn't she run off with some man?" Darby asks. "I heard that she took off with some professor and didn't come home for fifty years."

"Forty," says Calvin. "It was forty years."

"I'd never run off from home," says Joe Ed. "Mercy

Hill, Kentucky, is God's country!" He leans back in the kitchen chair until it touches the wall and his legs are dangling. Joe Ed is small for a football player and the coach never puts him in to play. Three years he's been carrying water to the players at time-out. Still, he thinks this place is the center of the universe.

"I might run off if the right girl came along," says Darby. "How about you, Chili? You wanna run away with me?"

The mixing bowl slips and I let some of the hard, dry beans go down the sink. If it stops up again, Momma will throw a fit.

"Darby!" Jack scolds his friend, and they all start laughing. "Chili's just a kid," Jack says. "She still plays with dolls."

"I do not!" I slam the lid on the bean pot.

When the boys get up to leave, Darby looks at me and winks. He has shiny black hair and dimples.

The four of them head down Persimmon Tree Road with a box full of chocolate bars to sell. Calvin hoists the box onto one shoulder and leads the way.

Miss Matlock never mentioned running away with a professor. She once told Willie and me that she had blanks in her mind, long spaces of time with nothing. The professor must be inside one of those blanks.

Uncle Lucius trots into the kitchen with his empty

fishing bucket and pole. Some days he's all there, and some days he's all gone. It's a hit-or-miss situation.

"Uncle Lu," I say, hoping this is a good day, "didn't you know Miss Matlock when you were young?"

"Oh yes," he says. "She ran away to see the world."

"With some professor, right?"

"Nope. He was a vacuum-cleaner salesman."

"No, no, Uncle Lu. That was Aunt Gretchen, for goodness' sakes."

Lucius stops in his tracks. "I do love Gretchen," he says.

"But what about Miss Matlock?" I say. "What do you know about her?"

"I don't love *her*," he says. "I know that much."

It's useless. I give up and go out on the front porch and sit in the swing.

In a while Aunt Rose comes and makes chicken and dumplings for supper so Momma won't have to cook after working all day. Myra gets back from Jellico Springs and waddles around the house smiling like she's got a secret. Nearly every day now she takes off to her house in Jellico Springs by herself to put up wallpaper or hang mobiles or organize the baby's chest of drawers, and then she comes back to our house to eat and sleep. She hums a lot to herself but doesn't write much in her poem book anymore.

It's almost suppertime when Jack gets back home. He crunches the empty candy box and throws it in the big trash can by the side of the house.

"We sold everything," he says. "That old crazy woman bought our last five boxes!"

When we start into the house, Uncle Lu and Lenny come traipsing through the living room. Uncle Lu's still carrying his fishing pole and Lenny has his bait bucket.

A few minutes later I look out the window and see them standing at the far end of the porch, where the sun's going down in a red sky above the mountains. Lenny holds the silver bait bucket while Uncle Lu casts his line into the jasmine bushes and catches blossoms.

 Bad Luck and Promises...

"The Matlock family got rich off the backs of miners," Rose says.

We're in the kitchen breaking green beans to can. The house is quiet, everyone gone in a different direction except the two of us. No one to say *Change the subject.*

"What do you mean, Aunt Rose?"

"Matlocks owned all the coal mines around here," she says. "They were a proud family, thought they were better than anybody else." She shakes her head. "Terrible stingy with their money, too."

Aunt Rose is a gossip. Can I believe everything she says?

"How do you know that?" I ask.

"I know," she says. "I know plenty more than I ought to be telling."

One minute I want her to tell me everything she knows about the Matlocks, and the next I'm not sure I want to hear another word. I want to be like Miss Matlock someday. I want to be someone who has been places and done things and lived out dreams. Still . . .

I remind Aunt Rose about that day last spring after Willie's grandmother died, when we were eating dinner and she said the Brights would have had money if old Mr. Matlock had paid Helena's pap what he owed him.

"What was that all about?" I ask her now.

"That boy's great-grandpa was the foreman of all these Matlock mines," she says. "He saw the miners being worked to death for pennies. Why, some days they stayed underground and never saw daylight."

"Why didn't he do something about it?"

"He did," she says. "He caused a strike that cost him his job. No place to work after that."

"Why?"

"The Matlocks owned everything back then," she says. "The only clothing store, the hardware, the movie theater. They had power over this whole region."

"How did they get to own everything?"

"Old man Matlock traveled all over eastern Kentucky making deals, cheating people out of their mineral rights. Paying fifty cents an acre!" Rose shakes her head and clicks her tongue with disgust.

"What are mineral rights?"

"It's what's underground," she says. "The Matlocks bought up everything underground even where other folks were living on top. People didn't know the difference, didn't see no harm in selling off what was under the ground. They had no idea that big companies could come in here and tear up everything to get to the coal."

Suddenly I remember that day helping Uncle Lu sort his lures and him saying Momma owned everything above the ground and under it, too, on Mercy Hill Mountain, and that for sure no strip-mining would be done on it. But Uncle Lu's mind comes and goes like the wind and you can't depend on everything he says.

"Uncle Lucius says the strip miners can't find work here because we own the mountain. Is that right, Aunt Rose?"

"Right as rain," she says. "Your grandma would turn

over in her grave if she thought that bunch was going to come in here and go to scalping our mountain."

Aunt Rose says that when the settlers first came to Kentucky, it was a wilderness paradise. People gardened and hunted and lived in peace, she says. And then coal got discovered and came up out of the ground like a rattlesnake, bringing pain and death and miseries of all kinds.

"Why'd the mines around here close down?"

"Too dangerous," she says. "And the deep coal seam run out. The good Lord put a stop to it."

"What happened to the old Matlocks?"

"They left town after all that striking business and their daughter, Elvira, running away and all," Rose says. "Went over to West Virginia to see what else they could destroy."

"How could those people be so mean?"

"People can be the cruelest animals on this earth, Chileda. You've got a lot to learn." Aunt Rose puts a kettle of water on to boil so we can have the canning jars scalded before Momma gets home.

"But Miss Matlock's not cruel," I say. "She's not like that at all."

Rose gives me her suspicious over-the-glasses look but doesn't say anything.

"I mean . . . she was a nice substitute teacher."

"Elvira Matlock ran away from it all," Rose says. "It's easy to run away."

"Maybe that was a good thing," I say. "If her family was so terrible, maybe it was good she got away from them."

"She was just like the rest of them," Rose says, "and she used poor Helena Wilkins to get where she wanted to go."

"What do you mean?"

The story is getting all tangled up, like all the other stories in this town, where everybody knows everybody else's business, where old grudges can spread down and get bigger through the years and make people hate each other without even knowing why.

"Helena was Willie Bright's grandma," Rose says. "She died last spring."

"I know that."

"Helena worked for the Matlocks even after her pap got fired. They kept her like a slave, doing the wash and ironing and cleaning toilets," Rose says.

"Some rich people do have maids. Maybe . . ."

"No maybes," Rose says. "I know what it's like to have to do up a man's shirt so it's perfect for some woman who's never dipped her own painted nails in starch. Besides, they didn't pay Helena enough money to buy groceries, much less do anything else. There are no maybes," she says.

"But how did Miss Matlock use Helena to run away? I don't understand."

"Promised her the world," Rose says.

"What do you—"

"Helena packed Elvira's clothes and slipped her off, walked with her seven miles in the middle of the night to someplace between here and Jellico Springs where that man picked her up."

"The professor?"

"I don't know who he was," Rose says. "Nobody knew him. Nobody except Helena. So that was the last of *her* job, too."

"Then why'd she do it? Why did she help Miss Matlock run away?"

"Elvira promised to send money and bring Helena to some fancy place in the city. She claimed they'd both be on easy street," Rose says. "Promises." She shakes her head. "Nothing but fairy tales."

"I can't believe Miss Matlock didn't keep her promise."

"Not one letter," Rose says. "Not one penny."

"Maybe there's a good reason," I say.

Aunt Rose sets the Ball jars in the sink and carefully pours scalding water in each one until it overflows.

I wait, hoping she'll say that she's not really sure about any of this, that maybe it's mostly gossip, that Willie Bright's family being poor has nothing to do with anything anyone has ever done to them. That it's just plain bad luck. Bad luck happens like lightning, without a cause or a plan or a cruel person to direct it.

"There are no maybes," Rose says again when the kettle is empty. "*Maybe* is a useless word."

Mrs. Bright, Whose Name is Amanda ...

At first I think it's a fox or a possum. No cars coming, so I walk out in the middle of the road, making a wide swing away from the ditch, away from the thrashing in the weeds. Walk faster but try to be quiet. It might have rabies.

When I look back to make sure nothing's following me, I see the pink dress with blue flowers. The head is downhill, hidden in the ditch, but the legs are jerking. The whole body is jerking. I hurry back. . . .

It's Willie's momma! Her eyes are rolling in her head and her teeth are clenched. They can swallow a tongue, Pop says. In a fit they can even bite it off.

I'm screaming but nobody can hear. Not a car on the

road and Mrs. Bright stuck in some horrible world of her own. I find a stick in the ditch and force it into her mouth above her tongue like Pop has said you're supposed to do. I scream and yell *Stop, stop, stop,* like Willie says his grandmother used to yell. But nothing helps.

When the blue jeep pulls up, she's already coming out of it, her legs with only little jerks, her eyes trying to focus.

A tall woman in bell-bottom jeans leaps from the car.

"Does she have her pills?" The woman bends over Mrs. Bright and calmly lifts her head onto a clump of crabgrass.

"Pills?"

"Her medicine. Does she have it with her?"

"I don't know." Willie never said his mother took medicine.

"Go get your mom's medicine now!" The woman shoos me away.

"She's not my mother," I say. "She lives in that white house on the hill. I don't think she has medicine."

The tall woman wants me to help get Mrs. Bright into the jeep, so I stand on one side and the woman stands on the other and we prop her up and she can walk a little, but she mostly leans on the woman, who is somebody I have never laid eyes on.

"We'll take her home," the woman says. "We'll find out why she doesn't have medicine for the epilepsy."

I won't get in the car. This woman is a stranger and I'm not about to ride with strangers. I point out the house again, just in case she didn't hear me the first time. I tell her I'm late, that I have to go home.

"Her name's Mrs. Bright," I say. "I don't know her first name."

Three times I walk back and forth up our lane between the road and the house. I look across the meadow and up the hill to the Bright house, see that blue jeep still sitting in the front yard. I stay on the porch for a while and then walk around the house, making a wide circle out to the edge of the garden, where the hollyhocks have grown above my head. They're top-heavy with big red blossoms, leaning over like they're about to fall.

The next time I look across the meadow, the jeep's in a different place. Where did that woman go? And why'd she come back?

After a while I see Willie come out on the front porch and I wave and take off down the lane. He meets me at the school-bus stop more out of breath than I am.

"Her name's Amanda," he says.

"Amanda?"

"My mom," he says. "That's her first name."

"Is she okay?"

"She's got pills now," he says. "That VISTA woman went to the Rexall and had some doctor order pills to make the fits stop."

This doesn't make one bit of sense. "Why wasn't she taking pills before?"

Willie shrugs. "We didn't know they had pills," he says. He looks down, moves his foot back and forth in the dirt like I've seen men stomp out cigarettes. "That VISTA woman says there's a lot we don't know. She makes you feel like a fool."

"Aunt Rose says the VISTAs think they know everything, but they're dumb as bricks when it comes to the ways of mountain people."

"I don't much like the VISTAs," says Willie.

I think about how everything works and doesn't work. The welfares and the regular people and the VISTAs. You can split the Mercy Hill people up like slices of pie. Every piece is the same but different. And forget about equal. Equal is something people just like to talk about. Still, that woman pulled up in her blue jeep at the right time. If she hadn't, Willie's momma might have never known about pills to stop the fits.

"You know, Willie, maybe the VISTAs aren't all that bad," I say. "So what if they know some things and we know other things. Maybe that's the way it's supposed to be."

He looks back at his house, shifts from one foot to the

other like he's getting ready to run a race. Disliking the VISTAs is something we all have in common. It's like everybody eating the same fried chicken for supper whether they live in the brick houses or the wooden houses or the shacks. Everybody eating except for outsiders. And nobody invites the outsiders.

I see the blue jeep pull out and start down the road. When it stops beside us, the woman leans out the window and tells Willie to go home.

"Your mother needs you," she says.

Willie straightens up; his face suddenly looks older.

The VISTA woman keeps hanging out the window, waiting, her blond hair pulled back in a ponytail, dark sunglasses sitting on her nose, and a smile so big it shows all her perfect teeth. Aunt Rose would say she's as pretty as a picture. But it's a picture that's out of place in Mercy Hill. It ought to be in a magazine.

Pills, Pills, and More Pills . . .

I head over to Miss Matlock's house an hour early, when I know Willie Bright won't be there. I talk to myself as I walk down the lane, remembering my conversation with Aunt Rose, and practicing what I'll say. *Why did you run away? What was the real reason? Why didn't you send for Helena like you promised? You live alone in this great big house and the four Brights live in a shack. Is that fair?*

She answers the door in her old blue robe.

"You're awfully early," she says.

"Just by an hour."

She looks at her watch and sighs, opens the door.

I follow her down the hallway with my hands in my pockets, my heart pounding.

"Chili, Chili, Chili!" Ivan the Terrible calls from the parlor.

"Good morning, Ivan." I wave to the parrot like he understands and he lets out a loud wolf whistle.

Miss Matlock pulls out a chair for me at the dining-room table.

"I'm a walking drugstore," she says, looking a little embarrassed. She takes several brown bottles from a plastic bag and lines them up at one end of the table. "I'll need a knife to cut the water pills."

I get up and go to the kitchen for a paring knife. When I come back, she's got the lids off all the bottles and the pillbox open. There's a row of slots for every day of the week—pills for morning, noon, and night and for one extra time in between, just in case.

"What's all this medicine for?" I ask. "I didn't know you were sick."

Miss Matlock has never mentioned being ill. This is the first I've seen of these pills.

"I'm not sick," she says. "I'm old. Old people take pills to keep ticking."

"Ticking?"

"This one," she says, holding up the smallest of the white pills. "It keeps my ticker running." She drops one white pill into each morning slot.

There are yellows and pinks and several other whites in different sizes and shapes. Pills for high blood pressure and arthritis and pain. A round red iron pill and a huge yellow pill that looks important but is only a vitamin.

The window's open and you can smell the just-mown grass.

"Why'd you leave Mercy Hill?" I ask.

"I left a long time ago."

"But why? Why'd you leave?"

"Wanted to see the world," she says.

"You didn't just want to get away from people? Some people?"

"Nope."

"You're sure?"

"I'm sure." She drops a pink pill in each second slot across the pillbox.

"Who'd you run away with?"

Miss Matlock stops counting pills and gazes out the window. "A man I loved more than the sunrise," she says at last.

"Who?"

"Just a man."

"Was he a professor?"

"Maybe," she says, smiling. "Perhaps he was."

Why is this old woman willing to talk about the tiniest incidents in her life but not willing to talk about the big ones? She's told me the smallest details about African dances, about the way the jungle smells when you first get up in the morning, about the cobalt-colored necklaces women wear in the desert to ward off evil spirits. Those beads were made from smooth stones, she once said. They felt like cool water.

"What about Willie's grandma?" I ask. "Why didn't you send for Helena like you promised?" I keep my head down and cut each water pill in half.

"I guess I forgot," she says finally.

"Forgot?" I look up and meet a blank expression.

"Sometimes when you're happy, there's no room for much else. It's easy to forget about other people."

"But it's not right."

"I suppose not," she says.

"You *suppose* . . ."

"It's a pity you can't go back," she says. "You need to

remember that, Chileda. You can try to make up for the past, but a person can never go back and undo anything." Little pools start to form beneath the blue of her eyes.

"Why'd you come back to Mercy Hill, anyway?" I ask. "If you were so happy, why didn't you just stay away?"

"Home is always home," she says. "Some people leave, some stay, some come back. That's how it works."

"But . . ."

"Remember the eels?" she says. "They always—"

"I remember the eels."

Her explanation is not the least bit satisfying. Questions pour through my head like a wild river. . . . I want to ask if the Matlocks really did get rich off the miners' backs like Aunt Rose claims, if her pap fired Willie's grandpa and made the Brights poor, if she ever feels guilty for using Helena Wilkins and then forgetting her. And that talk about change? What would she go back and change if she could? The words float in my mind like loose tree limbs in the river after a storm, refusing to come together.

"You'll leave, too," Miss Matlock says. "When you're grown up."

"How do you know that?"

"I know. Someday the world will open up and start calling to you."

A strong slant of morning light comes through the

dining-room window and in it Miss Matlock looks old. *Really* old. Older even than when I walked in the front door a few minutes ago. I only notice now that her blue robe is dirty, the buttons missing. Her hair hasn't been combed. I try to picture her as a young girl, walking away from Mercy Hill in the middle of the night with a man she loved better than the sunrise, giving up and forgetting about everybody and everything she'd ever known. Was it courage or craziness or anger? Or maybe all three?

She fumbles with the pillbox, trying to snap shut the little compartments.

"Wait!" I reach over and touch her bony wrist, feel her pulse race. "You forgot the water pills."

I drop the half pills one at a time into the night slots.

Crazies . . .

She died in her sleep. Dr. Smith, who's going to deliver Myra's baby when it gets ready to come, said it was heart failure that killed Miss Matlock. She went fast, he said. Didn't feel a pain.

How does he know?

The Reverend I. E. Fisher Jr. won't be preaching a funeral, and her body will not be put on display in that house, and there won't be any singing of "Amazing Grace," which is standard practice in Mercy Hill. Miss Matlock wrote up orders to the contrary. Momma and Rose are discussing this at the kitchen table before supper. Miss Matlock will be sent up North somewhere to be cremated and put up in a jar like preserves, Aunt Rose says. This is what Rose heard from one of the men who brought his shirts over to be washed this morning. A nephew of that old professor Miss Matlock ran off with years ago is going to take her to the jungle in a jar and throw out the ashes.

"In a jungle?" Momma shakes her head and clicks her tongue.

"For the snakes to get, I guess," Rose says.

"What would make a person want to be put away like that?" Momma asks.

"Craziness," says Rose. "Pure craziness."

Uncle Lu walks into the room as if on cue.

"Gretchen died," he says. His eyes are full of water and he looks from Momma to Aunt Rose.

"No, Lucius. Gretchen didn't die." Momma pats him on the arm. "We're talking about Elvira Matlock."

"Gretchen's fine," Aunt Rose says.

"She is?" Uncle Lu holds on to that one thought. "When did you see her?"

"We didn't see her, Lu. But she's okay," Momma says. Momma talks extra loud now when she speaks to Lucius, even though he has no problem hearing. She could scream and he still wouldn't understand.

"Elvira Matlock was a crazy woman," Lucius says.

"That's right," says Rose. "She didn't have a good mind."

Momma shushes him out of the room. "Get ready for supper," she says.

The minute Uncle Lu leaves, Aunt Rose bends over and whispers to Momma.

"Poor old fool," she says. "Wonder what makes a man get like that?"

"Aunt Gretchen left him," I say. "It drove him crazy." At least some things have answers.

"Chileda, go wash your hands," Aunt Rose says. But it's not even time for supper.

What's Left...

Miss Matlock left me her books. Some of them went to the public library, but the ones I enjoyed the most, the books about other places, she left to me with a note that said *Please share with Willie.* She was afraid they might get destroyed at Willie's house, she said, but I didn't tell Willie that part.

Jack and Lenny help me load the books in cardboard boxes. It feels strange being in that house without Miss Matlock. It still smells the same, and the professor's nephew has left everything in place like it's waiting for her to come back any minute. Everything, that is, except the birdcage, which is now sitting in the backseat of the man's red car. He says he's taking the parrot up North to live. I imagine Ivan looking out the window at piles of white snow and wondering what on earth happened to the world.

I sweep my hand across the back of the velvet parlor sofa and close my eyes. It could almost be any other summer day with Miss Matlock in the kitchen baking cookies. Any minute she might come down the hall with a pot of tea and those little cups that tinkled like bells when the sugar spoon touched them, pull a book from a shelf, and take us to the other side of the world. But not today. Not any day ever again.

When we get home, we put the books on the wide shelves in the smokehouse.

"They'll have to be moved when we kill the hogs," Pop says.

Every autumn, the hams hang from the rafters and

side bacon is salted down on these shelves. I'll have to find another place for three big boxes of books. Momma already said no to the living room and it looks like Uncle Lu will be in the attic until he has to be sent to the crazy house. Maybe when Myra leaves and takes all of her stuff, I can line my walls with books. I'll make it like a real library, a library in my own room, all smelling of books and filled with mysteries.

Nobody asks questions or says anything about Miss Matlock leaving me those books until suppertime. And I'm expecting it. The supper table is where everything gets discussed.

"I can't understand why she left those books to you, Chili." Momma holds her fork in front of her like she's concentrating on it instead of me.

"I like to read," I say.

"But . . ."

"She was my substitute teacher last spring. Remember?"

"Did you ever go to that house?" Pop asks.

"Today," I say. Not a lie, but not the whole truth.

He looks me straight in the eyes without blinking. "I heard down at Brock's store that several people saw you coming and going to the Matlock house practically all summer."

"And why would they be telling you that now and not before?" I say.

"Don't sass," says Pop, wagging his finger at me. I can tell he means it.

"You know how people are," Momma says. "They don't like to interfere, don't say a thing, unless it seems important."

"But they gossip plenty," I say. "They just don't tell the person they're gossiping about."

"That's enough," says Pop. "No need to make things worse than they are."

"Things are not bad," I say. "There's nothing bad at all." Except Miss Matlock's gone. I think it but don't say it.

"Well," he says, "I'll have to look at those books before you read them." He wants to make sure they're appropriate.

"I've already seen them!"

"Doesn't matter," says Pop. "Does not matter one iota."

"She needs to be reading the Bible," Uncle Lu says. Words of wisdom coming from a man who's drinking his coffee with a straw. Uncle Lu will no longer put his lips to cups. For three weeks now he's used straws for everything.

"I do read the Bible," I say to Lucius.

"Then you don't need other books," he says. "The devil hides in the pages of books."

I'd like to lock him up in a library and throw away the key.

California Dreamin' Like the Old Song . . .

Pop sits on the foot of my bed looking as pale as he did the night Uncle Roscoe died.

"I've looked through the books," he says. "I guess it's all right for you to have them."

"I've already seen them anyway," I tell him again. "Front to back."

Pop looks up at the light and blinks his eyes, sucks on his lips like he's trying to keep a jawbreaker from slipping out of his mouth.

"The people in those books are not like us," he says.

"They're real pictures," I say. "Real places."

Pop looks irritated. "I know they're real places, Chileda. But trying to go to these places, to run off . . . that'll get you in trouble. Just like it did Elvira Matlock."

"Miss Matlock never talked about any trouble it caused."

"She wouldn't," Pop says. "What didn't hurt her she didn't notice. But the others . . ."

"You mean Hel—" I hold my tongue. No use letting Pop know that I'd gossiped about all this with Aunt Rose. "I mean, what others?"

Pop doesn't seem to notice my slip. "Will Epperson, for one," he says.

I ask why Miss Matlock's travels could possibly have bothered Mr. Epperson.

"She was supposed to marry him," Pop says. "Then she up and runs off with some professor from Jellico Springs College and don't come back for fifty years."

"I thought it was forty," I say.

"Thirty, forty, fifty. What's it matter? She left Will, made a fool of him."

I picture old Mr. Epperson with his shiny bald head sitting in the back of Brock's store playing dominoes with Mr. Becker and Little Clyde Cummings. Every time the old man loses a game, he slams his fist down on the table and makes everybody jump. "Maybe she didn't like him," I say.

"Old Will's a good man," Pop says. "That woman couldn't have found anybody better." Pop's face has turned a raw-looking red.

"She must have."

"What?"

"The professor must have been better."

Pop's face goes white again and he pats me on the foot.

"She was a floozie, Chileda. And I don't want you following the ideas of some floozie."

"How do you know Miss Matlock was a floozie?"

"A man knows a floozie when he sees one," Pop says. He says he's seen this happen too many times. A woman gets it in her head to leave the hills, and she comes back a floozie.

"Who else?" I say, expecting Pop to mention Aunt Gretchen, except she's still gone.

"Roxy March," he says. "Nothing but a floozie."

I remember Roxy March coming back to Mercy Hill for Uncle Roscoe's funeral, carrying the big green reptile pocketbook.

"She was a good woman," he says, "until she went off to Cincinnati. And Dorcas Billings," he says, "you couldn't even recognize her when she came back from Detroit."

"That's because she lost seventy-five pounds," I say. I remember when Dorcas Billings substituted in my first-grade class and the boys called her the Blimp.

After a few minutes the hard edge slips out of Pop's voice and he starts stroking his chin whiskers.

"I once wanted to go to California," he says.

"You did?"

"When I was a young man, California was all I could think about."

"Why didn't you go?"

Pop says something happened that kept him here.

"What?" I ask. "What happened?"

"Life," he says with a sad little laugh. "I was meant to be here and life kept me here."

"I don't understand."

"You'll understand someday, Chileda. When it happens to you. You'll get all riled up and raring to go and something will happen to keep you here because this is where you're supposed to be. It's where you belong."

I don't have the heart to tell Pop that I've never belonged in Mercy Hill, that I've dreamt for a long time of belonging to a bigger world, that Miss Matlock just showed some of it to me, that's all.

"People come back," I say to Pop. "Miss Matlock went away, but she came back."

He sits for a while and stares out the window at the full moon. He's finished talking, but something hangs in the air between us.

"Do you ever wish you'd gone to California?" I ask Pop.

He pulls at his whiskers and shakes his head. "No need wishing," he says. "A wish in one hand and a nickel in the other won't even buy a piece of bubble gum."

Pop laughs for the first time all night. And I have to laugh, too, even though I feel more like crying.

 nder the Bleachers ...

Jack gets his new football uniform for the season. Number forty-five. He struts around the house in his shoulder pads and knee pads and stomach protectors, telling me to hit him as hard as I can in the belly. "Go ahead," he says, grinning at me. "I won't even feel it." So I wind up and hit him and he stands as still as a maple tree and just laughs.

Summer's about gone. Jack says he can smell football weather in the air. He leaves early in the morning for practice and stays all day. I follow him to the door and sniff the air, but I don't smell anything different.

Friday night everybody except Lenny and Uncle Lu goes to the first scrimmage of the season: Mercy Hill versus Jellico Springs High. I don't much like watching football, but Momma insists that I go to this first game. Even Myra waddles along with us in her flowered muumuu and slip-on tennis shoes. Her regular shoes won't fit anymore because her feet are so swollen her ankles have disappeared. That's what happens when a

baby is coming, Momma says. Babies put you all out
of proportion.

School won't start for another week, but they still
have the big lights burning on the field and popcorn at the
concession stand. Momma and Myra plop down on the
first row of bleachers, but I keep climbing all the way to
the top. I see Ginny and Priscilla down on the field talking
to the high school cheerleaders and some of the older
boys. They look like strangers.

At halftime I go for a Coke, but the snack line is too
long, so I go back to my seat and wait. When the third
quarter ends, I head again to the concession stand, slipping
behind the bleachers in the dark so I don't have to walk in
front of people. In patches you can see up through the legs
and feet to the lights. There are Coke cans and cigarette
butts and candy wrappers lying all over the ground. I'm
looking down at all this trash, wondering who's going to
clean it up, when I run smack into Zeno Mayfield.

"Whoa, Chili Pepper! Where're you going in such
a hurry?"

"To get a Coke," I say. I can smell Zeno's grape bubble
gum, but he's standing in the shadows and it's too dark
to see his eyes.

"Want a drink of mine?"

He sticks a cup in front of my face and I think about
it for a second. Why not? The line at the concession

might still be too long and I'm dying of thirst. I put my mouth right where Zeno's mouth has been and take a long swallow. It feels criminal.

The next thing I know, I'm beneath the bleachers getting kissed by Zeno Mayfield. His lips taste sweet with grape-flavored bubble gum and he kisses me hard like he never wants to let go. Finally, he leans back against the bleachers and I can see his face in a streak of light sliding down between the rows, smiling like a satisfied dog.

I study his eyes. Would that pair of eyes ever want to see the other side of the world?

"Zeno," I say. "Would you like to go to Paris, France?"

"Ummm," he says, like he's just bit into a Hershey's bar. He leans over to whisper in my ear. "Yes, yes," he says. "Take me to Paris." He closes his eyes and waits.

I lean up against Zeno's wobbly knees and kiss him back even better than he kissed me, long and hard like the French people kiss, like I've read about in Aunt Rose's *True Confessions* magazines, a kiss that Zeno could never have imagined I had in me.

He swallows his gum.

By the time I get back to the seat with my popcorn and Coke, the game only has two minutes to go. I sit and stare at the ball field but don't see a thing. Would it be so bad to fall in love with somebody and live forever in Mercy Hill?

A full moon hangs over the mountains, round and

cold and white like a Chinese paper lantern. I look down through the spaces in the bleachers and my head starts to spin. Miss Matlock's voice whispers on the night air: *Someday you'll leave . . . when the world opens up and starts calling to you.*

Birthday Presents...

At Brock's store I pick up three cans of Prince Albert loose tobacco for Uncle Lu's birthday. He rolls his own cigarettes. First he flattens the white tissue and spreads a pinch of tobacco on it, and then he rolls it up, licks, seals, and twists the ends until they're tight. He pops it into his mouth and lights up. Puff, puff, puff. Yuck!

Mr. Brock shakes his head at me, says he can't sell tobacco to a kid, even though he knows full well it's for Uncle Lu's birthday. So Momma has to get out of the car with her feet hurting and curlers in her hair and come into the store to pay for it.

She throws Mr. Brock a hateful look and says maybe next time we'll buy our tobacco in town.

"Don't make me no never mind," he says.

What kind of talk is that?

Next stop: the Holey Roller Donut Shop. Uncle Lu's favorite place sells doughnut holes only. It's typical of Mercy Hill to have a doughnut place that does not even make doughnuts. One day Uncle Lucius said to me, "How do they get the holes without the doughnut?" I had no idea how to answer that one.

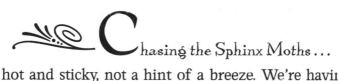Chasing the Sphinx Moths...

It's hot and sticky, not a hint of a breeze. We're having a barbeque to celebrate Uncle Lu's birthday. He says the Bible promised us three score and ten years and now he's reached it; he's seventy. So he's got to think of some way to pay back the Lord for every extra moment. Our yard is full of Os. Momma rented plastic folding chairs from the Osborne Funeral Home and every chair has a big white O on the back. The whole church has been invited to Uncle Lu's party because Pop says by next year he may not even recognize himself, much less all these other people.

Jack and Lenny set up the tape player on the back screened porch and you can hear gospel music from one end of the yard to the other. Uncle Lu said no rock and roll. Since it's his birthday, he can do whatever he pleases and he doesn't want to have to listen to the music of the devil.

I'm looking out the bedroom window when Uncle Lucius comes around the corner of the house pushing the wheelbarrow. He's been stoking the barbeque fire with big slabs of wood. Even though it's his birthday, he insisted on building the fire. Momma worried that he might get burned, but she let him do it anyway. You can't tell a seventy-year-old man what to do, she says.

Beyond Lucius's white head the sun is falling behind the mountains, turning the blue sky orange through the wood smoke. A snowy contrail cuts the sky in two behind the tiny dot of a silver plane.

All of a sudden Uncle Lu moves to the side and I see what's in the wheelbarrow.

No!

No!

I try to scream, but the words go silent, trapped in some deep, soundless place. My stomach winds up like a ball of yarn.

Nothing to do, but . . . stare at the fire, feel the heat of the words burning.

Lit pieces of paper float into the trees like fiery gems. Pieces of rain-forest rivers and blue Antarctic ice and snow-covered volcanoes.

Amongst the trees the men talk, pat backs, shake hands. Somewhere a woman with a sad voice sings "In the Sweet By and By."

I look up, fix my eyes on the orange sky above the fire, and watch the airplane dot slip farther and farther away. If only I could catch it. If only I could fly away from here and never come back.

I rush down the stairs in my black patent-leather shoes and new blue dress. Cross the sunporch. Slam the back door. Don't stop, don't speak, don't listen.

You look pretty tonight. Shouts and smiles and empty faces.

At the edge of the woods the trees are enormous umbrellas, casting shadows and shade. Thick vines full of orange trumpets, blue morning glories, all wild and winding into the trees.

Everything is a blur behind me. The stretch of green lawn, the house drifting farther away, people and cars and gospel music and chairs stamped with big white Os.

Two birds hover above the trumpet flowers. No, sphinx moths. Buzzing like tiny helicopters, revving their engines one second and *zip*, they're gone. Lenny says that's how it's done. That's how you leave. Wait until the time's right and *zip*, you go.

I run after them, last light falling through the trees, running and running into deep woods, where everything's dark and quiet. The moths disappear in the darkness, go wherever moths go for the night. I can't see the yard or the cars or the house anymore, but I keep running, blackberry briars and cockleburs catching onto my clothes, on and on up the mountain.

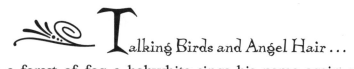

In a forest of fog a bobwhite sings his name again and again. *Bob whieeeet, Bob whieeeet.* It's like he can't stop. Pieces of pink light drop on the morning dew. I recognize the parlor that hasn't been a parlor since my momma played here, since everybody left and the walls crumbled and the floor fell through and the milkweed started growing.

Little cocoons of silk. Angel hair. *Crack the cocoon and scatter the angel hair in the wind.* It'll go wherever the wind takes it, wherever it wants to go. I want to go with the angel hair. I want to be scattered in the wind. I close my eyes to the pink light.

Chilleee! Chilleee!

Why is the bobwhite calling my name?

I open my eyes again and try to focus, see the sun

sliding up over the trees, my face in the rotting leaves, legs curled up like a baby. How did I get here?

. Slowly, the pictures come like a movie, marching one after the other, a parade of faces and hands and voices. The yard filled with people and music. The dogs barking. That awful scent of burning paper. My dreams, the pictures of my dreams, all going up in smoke. Miss Matlock gone and the books gone and I'm caught. Caught in the wind of this valley like everybody else.

I lie in the place that used to be the parlor of the old house on Mercy Hill and look at the weeds and the rotten boards and the old stone foundation in piles of loose rocks around me. I ran away. . . .

But this is as far as I got.

"Chili!" The bobwhite calls from somewhere close by now. But . . . bobwhite birds can't talk.

Shadows shift amongst the trees. First a red cap. Now a blue dress. A Sunday suit. My head spins.

The Reverend I. E. Fisher Jr.'s blue shirt that Zeno's little brother spit up on hovers in a blur above me.

"Look at her head. . . ."

"Must have hit it on that rock . . ."

"She's waking up. . . ."

"Thank God she's okay." ·

That shirt, the very one we wanted to see on a monkey, is now wrapped around my head, its sleeves tied

together and dangling at my ears. The preacher leans
close with his coffee breath.

"You're going to be okay," he says. "We're all here."

Cold water runs over my head and into my eyes and
I slip off, dream of big white birds in purple trees and a
red sky like Lenny says the sky is on Mars. People birds
chant my name over and over, coo and flap their wings
in my face, and the wind smells like . . . fried chicken?

When I wake up for real, they're all in the parlor, sitting on the rock piles and rotted boards and the hard
ground. Sitting amongst the milkweed. Eating chicken
and corn on the cob. Holey Roller doughnut holes in cinnamon and powdered sugar and chocolate are piled in
baskets on a tree stump and Frances Perkins is standing
over the sweets with a paper fan, keeping the flies away.
Quilts on the ground and kids on the quilts and women
running back and forth like the women always do, trying to make everybody happy. Off in the distance, under
the poplar trees, the men laugh and smoke. I can see the
lit ends of cigarettes moving in the morning mist.

Uncle Lu's bent over his walking stick, making his
way toward me through the weeds. I hate him, hate
him, hate him! He looks down at me and grins, his old
mouth empty.

"Lu lost his false teeth last night," Momma says from
somewhere behind me. I recognize her hands now rubbing

my head at the sore spot. "They dropped out when he fell," she says. He thought he'd found me, but it was just some old blue jacket hanging on a tree limb. It was too dark. "He stumbled," she says, "but can't remember where he was."

My crazy uncle is toothless because of me. The reverend's blue shirt is ruined, stained with blood because of me. The party is a day late, a dinner on the ground at breakfast time. All because of me.

Uncle Lu bends over in my face, spits when he talks, and I turn my head away from him and shut my eyes.

"What a birthday!" he says. "You made a good celebration."

I *want* to hate him. I want to be happy that he lost his false teeth and will look like a frog trying to eat without them. But how can you hate somebody who by next week probably won't even remember what he's done?

"You'd better eat some," Aunt Rose says. "Get something in your belly."

She steps over a loose board and hands me a paper plate with fried chicken and green beans and corn on the cob. There's garden relish, too, and sliced tomatoes and a chunk of Frances Perkins's homemade sunflower bread.

But I can't eat for crying.

No, I'm not hurting anywhere. I'm not mad. Not sad. Not worrying about anything. No. No. No. Really. Everything's okay.

And it is.

To Come and Go Like Magic...

Where do the ducks go when they fly in a V over the houses and trees and mountains? South, Aunt Rose says. They're flying away from the cold. Ducks are smart and ducks are free.

"Don't you wish you were a duck?" Willie Bright says.

"No," I say. "Why would I want to be a duck?"

"To be free," he says. "To fly south."

"I don't want to go south," I say. "I want to fly across the ocean."

"Ducks can't do that," he says. "They have to eat."

We're walking down Persimmon Tree Road with no place to go. A second flock of ducks quacks overhead, flying low above the treetops. This morning Aunt Rose said they were getting their bearings, so when the time's right, they'll be ready to hightail it out of here.

I tell Willie a story Miss Matlock once told me about

the monarch butterflies. I tell him how they fly all the way to Mexico in the winter and millions of them fill the trees, so it looks like the mountainsides are on fire. They stay perfectly still until sunrise and then they fly up in a great orange cloud. A "swirling wind of wings" is how Miss Matlock described it. Nobody knows when they go or how they know to come back. They just do. Spring comes, the flowers bloom, and the butterflies appear like magic.

"I wish I could be like a butterfly," I say. "I'd like to come and go like magic."

By habit we slip through the boxwood hedge and cross the yard. Miss Matlock's house is locked up tight. We stand on the porch and look in the window at the dark, lifeless parlor, the bookshelves empty.

"We can always get books at the library," Willie says.

"They're not the same," I say. "She had stories to go with all those places and pictures."

"We can make up our own stories," he says. Willie Bright would say anything to make me feel better.

"But we've never been anyplace. Not for real."

I walk to the end of the porch and sit sideways in the swing; I stretch out my legs and my heels slip over the edge. At the beginning of the summer my sandals fit smack against the arm of the swing when I sat like this. I guess I got taller without even noticing.

Willie Bright sits down on the top step in his usual spot with his back against the white wooden column.

"Miss Matlock left me some money," he says. Just like that, like this is plain old talk, news I already know—which I didn't.

"For what?" I ask, trying to sound just as everyday, *so what,* as he sounds.

"To go to college."

"College?" I'm looking straight at the worn-down bottom of Willie Bright's left shoe where a hole is starting to form, wondering what on earth Miss Matlock was thinking.

"Just for one year," he says. "Then I have to make the grades to keep on going."

"But you could spend that money for whatever you want."

Willie shakes his head. "The judge read us the will," he says, "and it's only good for school."

"That's not fair," I say.

"Maybe Miss Matlock didn't know how to be fair," he says.

"What do you mean?"

"When she ran away from Mercy Hill, she promised to send for my grandma," he says. "But she never did."

"I know."

"They were friends. Miss Matlock and Granny."

"I know."

"Who told you?"

"Aunt Rose."

"Did she tell you that Miss Matlock's professor liked my grandma first?"

"No," I say. Could this be true?

"Granny met him at the market. She was buying meat to make pot roast for the Matlocks and he was buying meat to make pot roast for himself."

"Really?" I imagine two people meeting for the first time in the meat aisle at the Piggly Wiggly, but back then there wasn't even a Piggly Wiggly. It was probably a little store on some street corner like Brock's.

"Grandma was a maid at the Matlocks'," Willie says.

"I know."

"Miss Matlock stole the professor away from her," he says. His eyes are empty-looking, but there's not one speck of anger in his voice.

"She did?" I wonder why Willie's grandmother would tell such a wild story. It doesn't sound like Miss Matlock, but neither does most of the other stuff I've learned.

"That's what Granny said," he tells me. "She met him first."

"Maybe that doesn't always mean anything," I say. "Meeting somebody first."

"Maybe not," he says. "But it ought to count for something."

"Why'd you go to Miss Matlock's house all those times?" I ask. "If you knew this, how could you still be her friend?"

"At first I was meaning to take something of hers."

"Like what?"

"I don't know," he says. "Something valuable. Something that would break her heart. Like she broke Granny's heart."

"Did you?"

"What?"

"Did you ever take anything?"

"Nope."

"Why not?"

Willie shrugs. "I don't know. Guess I don't steal."

"I guess you don't."

I hear a car in the distance and I stand up and look over the azaleas.

It's Pop! Coming home in the middle of the day and driving like he's on a coon-dog chase. Something is wrong. . . .

I hurry down the steps and head for the house, leaving Willie Bright standing on the porch with his hands in his pockets.

 oday Everybody Smiles ...

Professor Drew Montgomery pecks on the nursery window trying to get the baby's attention. He smiles and the baby smiles back. Baby Sam likes you, the nurse says to the piano-playing hippie professor from Jellico Springs and Wisconsin.

"He probably peed," the professor says. "One-day-old babies don't smile."

The nurse gives him one of those *you think you're so smart* looks, but the professor doesn't even pay attention. He just keeps on smiling at the baby.

When we get to Myra's room, I tell her I'll help. We can put baby Sam's bassinet on my side of the bed. But she says no. She's taking him to Jellico Springs the minute she gets out of the hospital. To his true home, she says.

"Don't worry," the professor says, "we'll take good care of him." Every head around Myra's bed turns and alights on this man in his ring-toed sandals.

It's just Pop and me. A nurse sent the boys home earlier, saying there were too many people in the room. Momma's staying now to help Myra with the baby. The professor's staying to help Momma with Myra. And Aunt Rose is staying to make sure nobody does anything she wouldn't do. It's just Pop and me to walk out the door of the hospital smiling to ourselves. Today everybody smiles.

 imes Change...

Times change. But you still love what you always loved—books and people and songs and pets.

Momma calls the baby Dumpling because he's pudgy and soft. Sam Dumpling has red curly hair and blue eyes, but Momma says all babies start out with blue eyes. Myra's eyes are brown and so are Jerry Wilson's, but Professor Drew Montgomery's eyes are that same hotflame blue and he has red curly hair, too, just like baby Sam. But I don't say anything.

Ginny and Priscilla have a group of new friends. They're all cheerleaders and they don't give the rest of us the time of day, but I don't care. That's how it goes.

I have things to do and places to go and people to meet. Well, someday, anyway.

Zeno Mayfield hung on to me like a leech the first week of school, saying he only wished that I was a cheerleader. It's hard for a boy like him to imagine being attached to some girl who is not now, and never will be, a cheerleader. I let him know, finally, that it was just a few kisses anyway, not even one quarter of a football game.

Every morning I cross my fingers and make a wish for Lenny. Next week he's trying out for *The Music Man* at school. If he gets a part and has all those other people to dance with, he won't need me for practice anymore, but that's okay. We all have our own ways to go—Lenny, Jack, and me.

The coach told Pop that Jack's on his way to a football scholarship, so Pop's really happy. He won't have to worry about college money for Jack. College is a big deal to Pop now, especially with a professor practically in the family. College was a dream for us before, Pop says, but who knows. Since Lenny doesn't play sports, he's counting on getting a scholarship for all the hard courses he's taking and the good grades he plans to make. That's the way to do it, he says. He can't imagine getting real money for dancing. But maybe someday.

For my thirteenth birthday I got a chocolate cake and an envelope. That's it. Nothing wrapped, no pretty ribbons. My heart sank. And then I opened the envelope and found a card that everybody had signed and a membership to the Five-for-Five Book Club. The first five books cost only one dollar each and then I have to buy one book a month at the regular price for a year. That's why everybody signed the card and that's why I got only one present. Each book costs between five and ten dollars, so they're all chipping in—even Uncle Lu. Pop says I can order anything I want. He doesn't even have to see the list. It's amazing what can happen between ages twelve and thirteen.

A few days ago a new family moved into Miss Matlock's house and they've already cut down the boxwood hedge and clipped the moonflower vines and made a brick sidewalk across the front yard. At night they have every light burning. Willie Bright says it looks like a hotel.

I don't see Willie much these days. He quit riding the bus after the first three days of school. At first I wondered if he'd dropped out like some of the other welfares do when they get to the upper grades, but then I saw him one day in the cafeteria. He told me the VISTA woman who'd helped his momma stop taking fits was giving him a ride. She tutors him in the library every morning, he said. Some days I see him across the schoolyard, rushing to get to class. If he sees me, he waves.

Times change. The people and the days swirl around me, and it seems like everybody has a direction and a plan but me.

September Light ...

Late September light is dimmer, yellow-white, the sky full of puffy clouds. The mornings are cool.

I walk out of general science and into the counselor's office. My heart races.

"I want to change my schedule," I say. "Switch to the hardest courses I can take."

"You'll have to do catch-up," she tells me. "It'll be a challenge."

There are papers to sign and a green slip to get me into the white house where the advanced classes are taught and where, my counselor says, I will embark on a new journey. I make a note to add *embark* to my word list and decide it's time.

The old white house sits at the corner of the school property. It has five rooms upstairs and five down, with plain wood floors and a separate little kitchen where you can eat if you bring your lunch. Students from two other schools in the district are bussed here to take classes.

Most of them will be strangers. I'll have no one to eat with or do projects with or call about homework.

My first class is pre-biology, Room 3, on the bottom floor of the white house. I wipe my sweaty hands on my sweater, leave the big red building behind, and follow a beaten path across the grass. Outside the classroom door I stop and take one last free breath.

The room is already full of students, five minutes early, in their seats and quiet. The teacher, another hippie-looking transplant from the North, looks up from her desk and motions for me to come in. My eyes wander around the room, passing over all the new faces.

Suddenly there's . . . Lily Lou Harris? The girl who took up for me that day we were jumping rope now looks up and grins. The next row over is Surry Nan Honeycutt in her faded dress and stringy hair and drooping eyes. Surry who sings must be smart, too.

The old house doesn't have lockers. Just a wall painted bright blue in the back of the room. In front of the blue wall where the lockers would normally be is the last row of seats. The last row where . . . It can't be!

Willie Bright with his bouncing eyes and bushy hair waves to me like I'm on the other side of the schoolyard.

So *that's* why he's getting tutored by that VISTA woman, that's why he had his nose in books all summer. Willie Bright's a sly fox, all right.

I follow the new teacher's flowing skirt to the empty seat behind Lily. After my knees stop shaking, I take out the slick new biology text and green composition book and smile to myself, but not so anyone can see. With this room full of brains I'm about to embark on a long struggle to make Cs. But, somehow, it feels like I'm right where I'm supposed to be, like I've already left Mercy Hill a little bit.

Lenny says that when he leaves he's going to take his Polaroid picture book so he can remember this place. Maybe Lenny needs pictures because he's not been here too long. But I've been here all my life. I can close my eyes and taste the watermelon split open on the picnic table or smell the sweet greenness of the cornfield after a summer rain. I don't need pictures.

I can leave Mercy Hill, but Mercy Hill won't ever leave me. Momma was right: these mountains will always be my true home.

Acknowledgments

My sincere thanks to the following people: Allison
Wortche, assistant editor at Knopf and Crown Books for
Young Readers, for her belief in my work, continued
support, and editorial expertise; a few special teachers
who brought the outside world to the mountains and
encouraged us to dream—Nannie McCormick, Edna
Evans, and Irene Hughes; and to my extended family
everywhere and the caring people of Appalachia who
help keep tradition alive and my roots intact.

About the Author

Katie Pickard Fawcett grew up in the hills of eastern Kentucky and spent two years as a social worker in Appalachia. She has counseled and tutored students in the Washington, D.C., area, written ads for the Peace Corps and VISTA, and worked for the World Bank, writing about development projects in Third World countries. Her personal essays have been published in several magazines, and her favorite diversion is travel and the different cultural experiences it brings. Ms. Fawcett lives with her husband and son in McLean, Virginia. *To Come and Go Like Magic* is her first novel.